I0626799

WITCH WAY TO HALLOWS' BAY

BRIMSTONE BAY MYSTERIES - BOOK 2

N.M. HOWELL

DUNGEON MEDIA CORP.

CHAPTER ONE

"I THINK SHE'S DEAD," A VOICE WHISPERED FROM above me.

I groaned, face plastered against the uneven wooden floorboards.

"Oh, shush," another replied. "Should we wake her up?"

I slowly opened one eye and strained to look up at the two blurry figures standing next to me.

"Oh, look, she's alive," the first voice said.

I squeezed my eyes shut, not quite ready to deal with the spinning world around me. My body ached, and my head pounded something fierce.

A toe reached out and poked me in the side. I groaned again, squeezing my eyes shut even tighter.

"Well, you can't stay there all day, River." I recognized Rory's voice.

I painfully turned my body over so that I was

staring up into the patterned plaster ceiling of 21 Black Cat Lane, my shared home for the past few months.

"Everything hurts," I groaned. I lifted my arm to cover my eyes as someone flicked the ceiling light on. "Turn that off, you witch."

I heard a laugh that I recognized as Bailey's. I squinted up into the blinding light above and made out the faces of two of my housemates looking down at me in mock concern. Rory and Bailey were witches like me, and we lived in this beautiful, albeit run down, Victorian mansion on the coast of Maine with Jane, my third housemate, and our pink-haired, pint-sized landlady, Mrs. Brody. Jane and Mrs. Brody were also witches, and between the five of us, my new cat, Soot, and the many ghosts that frequently made an appearance in Mrs. Brody's basement apartment, the house was full to the brim with magic and mischief.

"Off, please," I muttered. The ceiling light felt like it was burning a hole through my brain.

"Well, based on the number of bottles scattered around the floor, I'm surprised you're even capable of speech," Rory laughed, poking me again with her toe.

Again, I groaned. I then started to become more aware of my surroundings, and slowly turned my aching neck to see the carnage that lay around me. The floorboards had been torn up, and wood splinters lay around me. My closet door was off its hinges and some of the trim board had been pulled away from the wall. A number of holes had also been made in the plaster walls, revealing thin strips of splintered lath behind.

"Oh, no." Memories of the night before came flooding back into my mind all at once.

"Have fun last night?" Rory asked, smirking down at me with her arms crossed in mock concern.

"I didn't realize we were renovating," Bailey laughed. "You should have told us. I would have bought some paint."

Both girls laughed and I shook my head painfully. The pounding in my temples was getting worse, and I shut my eyes again as the room began spinning once more.

"What were you doing?" Rory asked.

I let out a loud sigh. "The stupid cat," I managed to say through my piercing headache.

"This cat?" Jane walked into the room holding Soot.

I immediately sat up and gaped at her. "Yes, that cat. Where on Earth did you find him?"

Jane raised her eyebrow as she pet the tiny gray fuzzball in her arms. "What do you mean, where did I find him? He was sleeping on the stairs like always."

I pressed the palms of both hands to my temples in an attempt to stop the throbbing sensation in my head. "No, no, no, no," I said, slowly shaking my head in disbelief. "Not possible."

"What are you talking about?" Bailey asked. "Why did you rip up the flooring?" She bent down to try and place one of the torn-up floorboards back into place.

"The damned cat," I said again. "He was in the walls. All night. He wouldn't stop meowing from inside the walls."

My three roommates stared down at me, their brows raised in unison.

"You sure you didn't just drink too much?" Rory asked. "Were you drinking absinthe, by any chance?"

"You are looking a little bit like the green fairy right now," Jane laughed. I felt nauseous and imagined Jane wasn't too far off from the truth.

"Definitely not," I snapped. "The cat was screaming from inside the walls all night long. It was driving me insane!"

The girls glanced back and forth at each other, then stared back down at me like I was some sort of unstable mental patient.

Suddenly, a meowing sound came from down the hall. Everyone turned to look in the direction of the noise.

"See," I said, crossing my arms stubbornly. "Not crazy."

Jane placed Soot on the floor, who immediately

sauntered down the hall to where the noise had come from. He walked up to the hallway closet, sat down, and looked back at us expectantly.

"Huh," Bailey said. "Maybe Mrs. Brody was right, and this house is haunted, after all."

"I don't think that's a stretch, considering she invites ghosts over to visit every other night," I muttered, then lay my head back on the ground in desperate hope that the room would stop spinning so violently around me.

Rory opened the closed door and the three girls leaned their heads in to inspect the space.

"Nothing in here," Bailey said.

Another muffled meow came from the closet.

"What the heck?" Jane said, walking up to the closet wall and placing her ear against the plaster. "It's coming from inside the walls."

"Told you so," I sang. I was quite pleased with myself despite the vicious hangover.

"Does anyone have a crowbar?" Bailey asked.

"In my room," I said, remembering that I had brought nearly the entire contents of the tool shed in last night to aid in my attempt to find the stupid cat.

Bailey grabbed the metal tool from my room and brought it to Jane, who immediately set to tearing out the trim board in the closet.

"It's easier to just smash it into the plaster," I said.

5

She popped her head out of the closet and narrowed her eyes at me, then shrugged. "Alright."

A loud bang emanated from within the closet a moment later, and then came the sound of splintering wood being torn out from the walls.

The meowing grew louder now that a hole had been put into the right wall. The poor cat was obviously stuck somewhere within the structure of the old house.

Soot meowed back, and Jane reached into the hole in the wall to feel around for the source of the sound.

After a few moments, she pulled out a little furry ball of black and white fur. "Aw, look, it's just a kitten," she said, lifting the cat up for all to see.

"How did you get in there, little guy?" Bailey asked, scratching the cat's ears.

Jane put the kitten down on the floor and it immediately pranced down the hall to me and climbed up to sit on my chest. It looked down into my eyes and meowed.

I stared back up at the little cat's light blue eyes.

"He likes you," Bailey said, coming to sit on the floor next to me to pet the cat.

"Sorry, buddy," I said to the kitten. "Already got one too many cats in this house."

Jane laughed. "Don't be silly. She's obviously already chosen you as her person."

"That's not up to the cat," I said. "People adopt animals, not the other way around."

"Tell that to the cat."

The kitten meowed again and pawed at my chin with its tiny little feet.

I sighed. "This is getting ridiculous. It's going to be a zoo in here."

Bailey beamed. "The best kind of zoo!" She tickled the kitten under the chin, who then rolled over onto her side on my chest and began to purr.

Soot walked up to the kitten and sat down next to me, watching its every move.

I heard another muffled noise coming from the closet and froze. "Did anyone else hear that?"

Bailey nodded. "Sure did."

Jane went back into the closet to inspect the source of the noise. "Can't see anything."

The noise sounded again, this time louder.

Jane let out a loud sigh and reached for the crowbar. She then began ripping out more of the plaster to make the hole bigger. After a few minutes, she reached into the enlarged hole in the wall and removed a rather large, fluffy white cat.

"You've got to be kidding me," I said, staring up at the large animal in Jane's arms.

She let the cat down on the floor, and it padded up to the kitten that was still sitting on my chest and began licking its face.

"Aw, it's the momma cat," Bailey squealed.

"Great, just great," I said, looking back and forth between the three cats sitting around me. "This is not happening."

"Looks like you got yourself a nice little fur family," Jane laughed.

I lay my head back down on the floor, giving up on any false preconceptions that this day may have played out to be just a normal Saturday.

Rory looked around the hallway and frowned. "We're going to have to do something about this before Mrs. Brody sees the state of the place."

Jane laughed, then looked over at Bailey. "You got this?"

"Yeah, yeah," Bailey said, her eyes remaining fixed on the kitten in front of her.

She lazily waved her left hand in the air, and the pieces of the house began to fly back into place.

"Wow, Bails," Rory said. "That's incredible. How the heck did you do that?"

Bailey shrugged, completely disinterested in the looks of awe that her magic had drawn from the rest of us. She continued to pet the kitten, already absolutely in love with the little thing.

"You should keep it," I said, picking the kitten up off my chest and placing it on the ground in front of Bailey as I sat up and leaned against the wall for support. "Keep all of them, actually."

The kitten immediately walked back to me and

stepped up into my lap. She then curled up into a ball and fell asleep. The mother cat curled up next to it and fell asleep as well. Soot just sat and watched them curiously, flicking his tail back and forth in silence.

"Nah, I'm pretty sure they've made up their minds," Bailey said.

I shrugged, then let out a sudden sneeze. I then glanced down at the cat on my lap and frowned. "If I'm allergic to you, I'm not going to be happy, cat." The kitten purred.

I sneezed again.

"Soot hasn't bothered you at all, has he?" Rory asked. When she noticed the expression on my face she immediately added, "In terms of being allergic, I mean." She knew how little sleep I got from that cat, as I was often grumpy in the mornings when we would all have coffee together. I hadn't slept well since Soot came into my life a few weeks back, as he loved waking me up in the middle of the night by pouncing on my face as if I were some sort of play thing.

I shook my head. "I don't think so, although, my allergies have been bad since I first got him. I just figured it was the dusty old house, though."

"Well, were your allergies bad the first weeks after you moved in?" Jane asked.

I thought about that for a second. "No, don't think so."

I stared down at the three cats in front of me with wide eyes. "Don't tell me I'm allergic to cats."

Bailey laughed. "Well, I don't think you have a choice either way. Once a cat has attached itself to you, there's no getting rid of it."

I sighed, then scratched Soot behind his ear as he brushed himself up against me. "If you're the reason behind my scratchy eyes, you're being put out on the curb," I said to the cat.

He meowed and flopped down on my lap next to the kitten, who was snoring lightly.

"Aw, it sounds like Mrs. Brody," Rory said, looking down at the cat in adoration. "How cute."

"What should we call it?" Jane asked.

I watched the tiny snoring kitten for a moment and pondered. "Agnes?"

The girls all laughed and it was decided.

"Agnes the kitten," Rory said. "Just don't tell Mrs. Brody."

We had learned our landlady's first name a few weeks ago when we had brought the ghost of a young murder victim home with us. She had made us promise to never call her by her first name, which we, of course, respected. But, you have to admit, Agnes really is a fantastic name for an old witch.

It's also a perfectly cute name for a little snoring cat.

I scratched the kitten's belly as it made little

snoring noises, and I could feel the rumble from the purring in her chest.

"What about the mom cat?" Bailey asked.

I glanced around the room to see if anyone else had an idea for a name, but everyone shrugged.

I sighed and reached out to scratch the white cat's ears. "Looks like you're just going to be known as Momma."

Momma purred and rubbed her back up against my arm on the floor.

Jane picked up a small empty bottle of spiced rum off the floor and held it up to me. "So, what spurred your binge fest last night?"

I sighed and closed my eyes as I leaned my head back against the wall. That was one part of the night I really didn't want to remember.

"You know Zack? The insufferable journalist I knew from NYU who came to help with the paper after the three murders happened at the beginning of the month?" I asked. Jane nodded and came to sit next to me on the hallway floor.

"The one who basically drove you out of your job and treats you like a bag of dirt?" Bailey asked.

I narrowed my eyes at her, then sighed again. "Thanks for reminding me."

"Sorry," she muttered.

"But, yes," I continued. "That's the one. I just found out he'll be staying indefinitely. JoAnn, my editor, has offered him a full-time position at the Brimstone Press."

"You can't be serious," Rory said. "So, what does that mean for you?"

I shrugged. "Not sure, but it's not good. Not only am I essentially demoted, but I now have to put up with his condescending and misogynistic attitude every day at work."

"Oh, let's curse him!" Jane exclaimed.

I laughed at how excited she sounded. Oh, how I wish I could curse him. "No, not just yet. JoAnn and Zack are doing the dirty – don't ask me how I know - and knowing Zack, I suspect he'll find some way to mess it up sooner or later. I just have to wait it out, and hope that JoAnn sends him on his way."

"Well, maybe you should have gotten into your editor's pants first," Jane said. "Then maybe you would have gotten the job instead."

Bailey smacked Jane on the shoulder but laughed just the same. "That's no way to get ahead in the workplace."

Jane winked at me and I groaned. "Well, technically I already had the job, but that's a whole other disastrous story."

Soot yawned and stretched on my lap, triggering my own loud yawn in the process. I tried to ignore the itchy sensation I could feel building in my eyes. There was no way I was going to allow myself to be allergic to cats.

I petted both cats that were lounging on my lap, then softly pushed them off onto the floor. They both curled up together and went back to sleep, completely ignoring the rest of us talking around them.

I pushed myself up off the floor and steadied myself with the wall as a wave of nausea nearly overtook me. I walked towards the large window that overlooked our front lawn, and lifted the heavy wood-frame window open. I then leaned out and breathed in the crisp late October air, and immediately felt better.

The trees had turned a beautiful golden orange and red, and the wind blew falling leaves around on the grass. I loved the fall, especially here in Maine. The colors were so vibrant and made the town glow a warm gold all season. It was much nicer here than in New York City, which was mostly just gray and dreary this time of year.

I took a few more refreshing breaths, then pulled my head back inside the window and went to join my roommates who were picking up the empty bottles in my room.

I helped them tidy, then sat on my bed, glad that it was now the weekend and that I wouldn't have to face Zack or JoAnn for another two days.

Until then, I could enjoy the beautiful fall weather, recover from my hangover, and lounge around with my randomly growing family of cats.

I laughed to myself, as I've never in my life been a cat person. Dogs, I liked. Dogs obeyed you and loved you unconditionally. Cats have a mind of their own, and I was never really fond of them.

That is, until now. I lay back on my bed and Soot jumped up to join me. Bailey picked up little Agnes and put her down next to me, then joined us at the foot of my bed.

The two cats curled up next to my face, taking up all the room on my pillows.

I nuzzled my face into the little kitten, then sneezed.

CHAPTER TWO

LATER THAT MORNING, I JOINED MY HOUSEMATES outside to help Mrs. Brody with the preparations for the upcoming Halloween celebration. Every year, she puts on a big party in the yard and down on the beach. It's the only time of year that she socializes with anyone outside of the house, and, as far as I understand, it's the only time anyone else is allowed on the property. Our yard was well suited for a party, with a large expansive lawn overlooking the bay. Every year around Halloween, the area gets the nickname Hallows' Bay because of the grand celebrations Mrs. Brody puts on.

Apparently, it was the party of the year, but that has yet to be seen. These people rarely traveled outside of town, so I was curious to see how it would compare to an actual city celebration.

Mrs. Brody was joined by Nancy Pots, the local

bakery owner and good friend to us witches. The girls and I spend a lot of time in her bake shop, chatting about life and testing out her latest creations. She was a fantastic baker, and everything she made was absolutely delicious. I put on at least five pounds since moving here because of that woman.

"Hello, dear," Mrs. Pots called out when I joined them outside. "Lovely to see you."

She pulled me into a big hug and squeezed me tight. She was a very maternal person, and it was a shame she didn't have any kids of her own.

"Who's watching the shop?" I asked as I bent down to help Mrs. Pots pick up a long string of lights.

"I closed the shop for a few hours," she replied, busying herself with untangling her end of the string. "Wouldn't want to miss the party preparations, now, would I?"

I laughed. "I wouldn't really consider party prep to be something to get excited about, but to each her own." I eyed her suspiciously, as in the few months I've lived in Brimstone Bay, I have never seen her close the shop down once.

I helped her untangle the lights, then we tied the strings up to the trees around the yard.

The decorations were looking great, and I could only imagine what the yard would look like at night when the lights were all lit.

"The yard is looking really good, Mrs. Brody," Bailey said through a mouthful of apple. There were large baskets of fresh apples scattered around the yard next to wide empty barrels. I imagined they were going to be used for bobbing for apples.

Mrs. Brody snatched the apple out of Bailey's hand and bopped her nose with the tip of her finger. "Those aren't for you, dear. Save some of the food for the guests. Besides, you don't want to get tubby, now, do you?"

Bailey touched her hand to her stomach and gasped. "It was just an apple!"

"Fruit makes you fat, dear" Mrs. Brody said matter-of-factly as she went back to puttering around in one of the many boxes she had spread across the yard. Bailey huffed and reached for another apple.

"So, what exactly do you have planned for the party?" I peeked into one of the boxes and noticed a bunch of strange metal knickknacks. I dug through the box, but didn't recognize any of the strange items. Various shapes were cut into metal pieces; some rolled into tubes and others welded together in boxes. Cats, pumpkins, stars, and other shapes were punched into the sides.

"Tonight will be just for us. We always get our own little party, first," Jane said as she and Rory came to join us. Both girls had gone down to the beach to collect firewood, and dumped their armfuls in a pile near Mrs. Brody. "Tomorrow, we'll party with the rest of the town. If they show up, that is. Hopefully, the Shadow Festival didn't scare them, too much."

I laughed. "From what I hear at work, everyone has been looking forward to this for months. Apparently, last year's party has left quite the impression."

Bailey beamed. "It is a really fun time. Everyone dresses up and there's lots of good food and drinks. I hired a band to come play tomorrow night as well, and everyone stays out until the sun comes up. It's almost like a yearly ritual."

"And what's tonight supposed to be, then?"

"Think of it as a sort of pre-Halloween," Rory said. "A chance for us to enjoy the holiday before all the crazy happens tomorrow night."

"More like a chance to practice and prepare ourselves for tomorrow," Bailey added.

I eyed her, not sure what she was implying. I had of course heard every rumor there was to hear about Mrs. Brody's Halloween parties. Brimstone Bay was, if anything, an excellent rumor mill.

"Just a small pre-party, dear," Mrs. Brody said, holding up one of the metal objects to inspect it. "Where are the cake displays?" she asked, turning to Mrs. Pots.

"Oh, shoot, I left them in the shop," Mrs. Pots replied. "I knew I was forgetting something."

"Better hurry up and get them, dear," Mrs. Brody

said to her, a stern look on her face. "We'll be needing them for the desserts tonight."

Mrs. Pots huffed, then turned to me. "You'll get them, won't you, dear?"

"Uh," I started. "I guess so?"

"There's a good girl," she said, walking over to me and patting my cheek like a child. "You run along, then, and pick up the cake displays. They're in the back room." She then placed her set of keys in my hand and turned to finish her work with the lights.

I glanced down at the keys, then stared back up at her. "I'll just be going, then?" I asked confused, and glanced over to Bailey. She shrugged back at me and took a bite of another apple.

"I should probably get some work done at the office today, anyway," I said. I was going to go ahead and expect a hangover the morning after Halloween, and it would be nice to have the event story written up at least partially before the weekend was over. It's never a bad thing to get a head start on work.

I left the women to their decorating and picked up my laptop in my room before going to find my bike at the side of the house. I had no idea why Mrs. Pots wouldn't go herself, but I figured I might as well make myself as useful as I could.

The bike ride into town only took about five

minutes, and I locked up my bike in the usual spot in front of Mrs. Pots' Bakery.

I grabbed the keys from my bag and was about to unlock the door when I heard a loud banging noise coming from partway down the block. When I looked to see what it was, I noticed Mr. Bramley's cafe, which was located just below the Brimstone Press office where I worked, had a big red closed sign on the door, and there were crazy loud noises coming from behind the boarded up windows.

Curiosity got the better of me, and I went to investigate what was going on.

I couldn't see through the door because someone had put up newspaper to cover the glass, and the windows had plywood boards behind them, covered in more newspaper. I recognized some of my articles.

I knocked on the door and waited for someone to come. The noise continued, and no one came. I could hear rock music blasting from inside, muffled by the sound of power tools, or something of the like.

I knocked harder this time and shouted through the locked door. "Hello! Mr. Bramley?"

After a moment, the music turned off and I heard the front door lock click as it unlocked. I stepped back, expecting to see Mr. Bramley step through the door.

I did a double take when Jordan O'Riley's face

appeared instead, beaming out at me like an excited child.

"Oh, hey, River." Jordan stepped out from the front door and pulled me into a big hug. I caught a small glimpse of the carnage that lay behind him, but realized I didn't care in that precise moment in time. His chest smelled like vanilla. I hugged him back, inhaling the intoxicating scent on his shirt as I pressed my face into his chest.

After a lingering moment, we both pulled away and smiled at each other.

"What are you doing here?" I asked, shaking my head incredulously. "Shouldn't you be back in Boston?"

I had met Jordan only a few weeks back when, unknown to me, he came to town undercover to investigate the bodies that had appeared during the Shadow Festival. I had ignored his advances at first, thinking him nothing but a thug who came to town to visit the guy who turned out to be the murderer. But after finding out he was actually a cop, it was hard to resist those adorable, piercing blue eyes.

He shrugged. "City life isn't for me, so I jumped on the opportunity when I could."

I raised my eyebrow at him, not following what he was saying.

"Didn't you hear? Mr. Bramley shut down the cafe permanently. He sold the shop to me for a really great price."

I gaped, unsure what to say. Of course, Mr. Bramley would want to get away, seeing as he just discovered his only son was a murderer. I didn't blame him for leaving.

"You bought the shop?" I managed to say after processing the information.

"Yeah," Jordan laughed. "Needed a change, you know?"

"Yeah, I get that. So, you're actually moving to Brimstone Bay?"

He nodded, smiling down at me with that winning smile of his. Crap, I was in trouble.

"Already moved. Gave my notice to the force two weeks ago and found a place in town right away."

I was still in disbelief. "Do you know anything about running a coffee shop?"

He laughed. "No, but I've partnered with my friend Trey from Boston. He's a pastry chef and is going to help me run the place. It's shaping up to be more of a dessert bar than a cafe, it seems, but I'm just going with it."

A loud bang came from within the shop and I jumped. Jordan quickly opened the door to look at what the commotion was, then laughed again. "Dude, leave the heavy work to me."

Jordan reached for my hand and led me inside the cafe. Or, at least, what used to be the cafe.

The place had been completely gutted. The walls

stood bare with the studs exposed, and the cafe counter and all the furniture was gone. It took me a moment to process the scene of sheer disaster that was in front of me.

"River, this is my good friend Trey Wong. He's a pastry chef from Boston."

I smiled and shook his hand. "Nice to meet you."

"Likewise."

"He owns the Desserti restaurants, if you've heard of them," Jordan said.

I gaped at him. "Desserti? Are you kidding? That's incredible – I love your food!"

I shook Trey's hand a little too frantically, then pulled my hand back embarrassed. His restaurants were legendary, and I'd been to the New York one with friends a number of times. When we could manage to get a reservation, that is. Desserti was one of the most successful restaurant chains around.

"Trey has restaurants across the country. Boston, New York, Seattle, and now, soon to be Brimstone Bay."

"That's amazing," I said to him, excited to be meeting the man responsible for some of the best food I'd ever eaten. "But, why Brimstone Bay?"

Trey shrugged. "City life gets old. Especially, in the restaurant business. I figured a small town would be a refreshing change. Besides, Jordan has a way of convincing people of things."

I grinned at Jordan. "Sure does." He winked at me.

"Ah, crap. Who the hell left all this garbage on the floor back here? I nearly tripped and fell on my ass," a female voice called from the back room.

Jordan grinned as a tall black-haired woman came in from the back room. "And this is Grace, Trey's wife."

"Oh. My. God! River Halloway?" The young woman lunged herself at me and pulled me into a tight hug.

"Grace?" I laughed into her hair. "Are you serious? What the hell are you doing here?"

Grace pulled back from the hug and waved her left hand with a big fat diamond ring in front of my face. "I got married!"

"I see that." I smiled. "Congratulations."

I studied with Grace's younger sister Emily at NYU, and the three of us would often go out clubbing together. Grace was dating a male witch at the time, and we spent a lot of time in the paranormal underground clubs. To be honest, she was the last person I expected to get married so soon.

"How's the restaurant going?" I asked her.

She shrugged. "Better now. Thanks to hubby." She walked up to Trey and put her arm around him. He smiled lovingly down, at her and I could tell he was completely infatuated.

Grace owned a small local New York restaurant that specialized in New York style cheese cake. Last time I was in town, it seemed to be doing well, but you never knew what went on behind closed doors, I supposed.

"When this big goof moved in a cross the street, his dessert shop started stealing all of my customers."

Trey blushed, then squeezed his wife back in their half-hug.

"Luckily," she continued, "fate brought us together, and we had the brilliant idea to merge restaurants. Now, the restaurant not only has the best cheesecake in town, but the best pastries, too!"

"Wow, guys, that's awesome," I said. "Congratulations."

"Thank you. I'm happy you guys know each other," Trey said. "I was worried Grace would get bored in such a small town after living in New York."

She shrugged. "I'll be fine. It's not for long, anyways."

Trey blushed again then looked down to his feet. "I was thinking we would stay, actually," he mumbled.

Grace stepped away from him. "Excuse me? That's definitely not happening, dear." Her emphasis on the word dear made it clear she was not happy.

Trey shrugged. "I think some quiet would be

good for us. All that stress of managing those restaurants is starting to make me lose my hair." He laughed and ran his hands through what looked to me like a glorious head of thick hair.

Grace rolled her eyes. "You're just lazy. We're on the way to being a global success, Trey. I know you're as excited about that as I am."

Trey shrugged then smiled. "Of course."

I stepped back from the couple and smiled. "Well, I should get going. It was great meeting you, Trey. Nice seeing you again, Grace."

I turned to leave and Jordan walked me out of the shop and closed the door behind us.

"I should probably leave those two alone for a few minutes," he said. "It's been nothing but bickering between them since they arrived."

I could imagine. Grace wasn't exactly an easy-going person. She was good fun during a night out, but she was high strung and had a hot temper. But you had to be a certain kind of person to run a restaurant in New York, I imagined.

"Yeah, better let them cool off."

I looked up at Jordan and he couldn't keep the smile off his face. "I'm just happy to see you, River."

"I'm happy you're here," I said quietly back to him. "Hey, we're having a Halloween party tomorrow night at the house. Want to come?"

"Yeah, Mayor Scott told me all about it. Apparently, it's the party of the year."

"That's what people say," I shrugged. "It's my first year, so I'm not sure what to expect."

"Are you dressing up?" he asked me.

I grinned. "Yeah, my housemates won't let me get away with not dressing up. You?"

"I'm sure I can manage something," he said. "What are you going as?"

"I was thinking of going as a witch," I said, laughing to myself. "Seems easy enough."

He laughed back at me, but a momentary look of unease flashed over his eyes.

I nudged him with my shoulder. "Don't worry, the party will be fine. Totally tame, no magic."

He smiled. "I'm not worried."

"See you tomorrow night?"

"You bet. Looking forward to seeing you as a witch," Jordan winked at me.

I smiled, then quickly turned to leave so he wouldn't see me blush.

CHAPTER THREE

I noticed the light on as I climbed the stairs to the second floor office of the Brimstone Press. I paused before opening the door and considered turning around and heading back to the house to work there, instead. I really wasn't in the mood to chat with JoAnn, and if Zack was in there... Well, even worse.

I sighed and resigned to going in anyway, as I knew I wouldn't get any work done at home with all the party preparations going on. The cats never seemed to let me work, either, preferring the warmth of my laptop keyboard to their own beds the majority of the time.

"Hey, kid," Zack said to me as I walked in.

Great. "Oh, hey, Zack."

Zack was sitting at his desk, which used to be my desk, next to the front window. He was typing away at some article or other. Nothing I would know about, as JoAnn seemed to be keeping me out of the loop these days. Ever since she offered Zack the job, I've been pushed aside like some forgotten puppy. I wasn't given an official demotion, but it certainly felt that way.

"What are you doing here on a Saturday?" I asked as I pushed some of JoAnn's things aside to clear room on her desk so I could work. The office was tiny, and not everyone had their own desk. Well, I did, not that I'm bitter about that or anything.

"Working on a few stories," he replied. "It's amazing how exciting things can be around here. So much to write about!"

I rolled my eyes as I rummaged through my bag with my back towards him. "Oh, yeah, sure." I brought out my headphones and pressed them tight into my ears so I could listen to music as I worked. Really, they were an excuse not to talk to Zack, but let's hit two birds with one stone with this one.

I tried to ignore him as I focused on my own work. I was tasked with writing up the article about the Hallows' Bay celebration, which was good as I could get the inside scoop from my housemates and Mrs. Brody. I was excited about it at first, but then when I realized I'd essentially have to be working throughout the duration of the event, I was less excited.

Hopefully, by typing out a bunch of stuff

beforehand, it would make the article much easier to write afterward. I really needed the weekend to unwind and let loose a little bit, and I didn't want to be focused on work the whole time.

"You excited for the Halloween party?" Zack asked me.

I pretended I couldn't hear him and continued typing away at my keyboard.

"I know you can hear me," he repeated.

I glanced up at him and pulled out the earbuds. "Sorry, couldn't hear you. What's up?"

"Your headphones aren't plugged in, you know."

I glanced down at the headphone jack on my laptop and saw that he was right. Well, crap.

"Sorry, just lost in thought," I said quickly, trying not to look like a complete idiot. "What did you say?"

"I asked if you're excited for the Halloween Party." He smirked and I could feel my face growing hot. Dammit! The last thing I needed was for him to think I was embarrassed. I was not going to let that man think he had any power over me.

"Yeah, I guess so," I shrugged. "Should be fun." I put my earbuds back in and turned my attention back to my laptop.

"JoAnn and I are really looking forward to it," he continued. "She's picked out a costume for me and everything."

I sighed, giving up my attempt at getting any work done.

"Oh, great. So, I'll see you there." I didn't even try to hide the annoyance in my voice. Zack knew full well what his coming here did to me. He had a perfectly good job at the university back in New York, and I suspected part of the reason he accepted the position, apart from his disturbing new relationship with my editor, JoAnn, was because he knew it would drive me mental. His misogynistic attitude towards the female students in his class and his sleazy attempts at flirting really put me off of him at school, and I never made any attempt to hide my feelings towards him. Or lack of, in any case. I felt like his attitude was some sort of cruel way of getting back at me for ignoring his advances and brushing him off as the pig-headed idiot he was.

"Looking forward to spending time with you tomorrow night," he said.

"Yep, ditto." I made no attempt to hide the sarcasm in my voice. I packed my laptop away in my bag and left the office without saying another word. I just really didn't have the emotional capacity to deal with him. Not after he took my job, wooed my boss, and made every attempt to ruin my life since coming here.

I paused to take a few deep breaths of the cool autumn air outside of Mrs. Pots' Bakery before going in to grab the cake displays she wanted.

Stretching my arms high above my head and closing my eyes, I inhaled and exhaled deeply, letting the motion relax me. After a few deep breaths, I felt better, and was ready to tackle the party preparations with the girls.

The display trays were scattered around the shop, but it didn't take me long to track enough down. They barely fit into the bike bags I brought, but I managed to somehow balance them all between the bags and awkwardly cycled my way back towards the house.

When I arrived, I began unloading the cake displays on a table in front of Mrs. Pots, who immediately busied herself with laying them out on the tables in a tidy order. She hummed as she worked, ignoring me as I placed the last of the trays in front of her.

"So, Mr. Bramley sold the cafe," I said conversationally as I watched the last of the decorations get strung up.

"What, seriously?" Bailey asked. She dropped what she was holding and stared at me. "Why?"

"I'm assuming he didn't want to be reminded about Ryan," I answered.

Bailey fidgeted with her fingers and stared down at her feet in silence. The poor girl was still taking it hard, and she didn't seem to be fully recovered from the events of a few weeks ago.

"So, does that mean no cafe?" Rory asked.

"He sold it to someone," I said, feeling my cheeks blush.

Rory raised her eyebrow at me and tapped her foot on the ground as she waited for me to continue speaking. When I didn't, she prompted, "…Who?"

"Jordan O'Riley."

"WHAT?" Bailey gasped, immediately cheering up. "Really? That hot cop?"

I laughed. "Well, I guess he's not a cop anymore. He's a restauranteur, or whatever it is they call themselves."

"So, the cafe will stay open?" she asked.

I shook my head. "Not exactly. He's turning it into a dessert shop."

A loud clang came from behind Mrs. Pots as she dropped what she was holding. We all started in her direction and she let out a loud *Hmph* noise.

"Did you know about this?" I asked her.

"Of course, I did," she snapped back at me. Mrs. Pots when turned to face us, a look of sheer anger on her face. "Those good for nothing city people bringing their fancy dessert shops to our town," she huffed. "They're going to put me out of business for good, that's what's going to happen. Curse the lot of them."

"Mrs. Pots," Jane gasped. "That's not very nice. Do you even know these people?"

"It's the same person who made the cakes that Mr. Bramley imported from the city. Mister Fancy-pants Wong and his outrageously overpriced desserts."

I walked over to her and placed a hand on her shoulder. "It's going to be okay, Mrs. Pots. They won't steel your business, I'm sure of it. I doubt there's a market for that sort of thing here, anyway."

"Besides," Bailey said. "You've got a loyal customer base, and you're the town's favorite baker, hands down. No competition."

Mrs. Pots sighed. "I still wish they would just disappear for good. That place has bad vibes written all over it. Bad spirits in there; I can feel it."

I noticed Mrs. Brody smirk, then turn to face the other way so Mrs. Pots wouldn't notice.

Mrs. Pots claimed she could speak to spirits, which we all dismissed as completely ridiculous as she's not a witch. Although, I had a feeling she had some sort of strange affinity for the otherworldly. How, I didn't know.

"I think the decorations are complete," Mrs. Brody chimed in. We all took in the incredible scene before us: the endless lights strung up between the trees, the decorated tables across the lawn, and the many baskets and barrels full of treats for everyone to share.

"It looks remarkable." I was in awe.

"Just you wait until tomorrow," she said. "This is nothing."

I raised my eyebrow but didn't say anything. I

knew better than to ask, and would just wait to see what sort of mischievous plan she had for the following night.

"Why don't we make a bonfire and all have a drink and relax?" Rory suggested.

"Great idea. I'll grab the ciders from inside." Bailey bounced off toward the house. The idea of a drink seemed really nice right about then.

Rory and Jane set about building a fire in the fire pit near the edge of the bluff, and I helped bring up a few chairs. The sun had nearly set behind the trees and the sky was glowing a deep purple color.

I sat down in a low-backed chair next to the growing fire and took in my surroundings.

Mrs. Brody had turned on all the lights and the rear yard simply glowed. The decorations were beautiful, if not eerie, and the lights created these flickering shadows across the grass.

"Oh, very cool," I said, noticing the strange little metal things I had found in the boxes earlier. They were light cases, and the shapes cut into the sides cast shadows on the surrounding areas from the lights set behind the metal. The effect was really cool, giving the impression that there were ghosts and other spooky things about. In truth, there actually were, but most people didn't need to know that.

Once the fire really started roaring, everyone took a seat around the perimeter and relaxed while

Bailey poured out the ciders and handed them to each of us.

"Well, you girls certainly have done well for yourselves here. This looks absolutely marvelous," Mrs. Pots said after a few long moments of silence when everyone simply took in the magic of the environment.

"It is something, isn't it?" Mrs. Brody answered, looking around proudly at what she had accomplished.

"Simply magical. You should all be so proud. Tomorrow will be an absolute treat."

"Mrs. Pots," I said, somewhat reluctantly. I then paused, not sure how to formulate what I wanted to ask her.

"Yes, dear?" The small plump woman looked over at me from her sunken chair.

"You seem awfully comfortable around people with magic," I said. "How did you come to be part of the community?"

Rory shifted uncomfortably beside me, and I could immediately tell that I may have asked something I shouldn't have.

"Sorry, never mind," I added quickly. "Didn't mean to pry."

"Oh, no, dear, it's perfectly all right," she smiled at me. "It's a good question."

She sat pondering for a moment, and we all

watched her in silence as she pieced together what she was going to say.

"It would have been my daughter," she said. "Or my husband, I guess."

"I didn't know you had a family," I gaped.

She sighed, a certain sadness filling up her bright eyes. "I did. Not anymore." She took a long sip from her glass of cider.

"You see, my husband came from a long line of witches. Showed no magical ability himself, unfortunately, but his whole family was full of witches and other such magnificent creatures. His sister, Twila, was astonishingly talented, though, and our daughter took after her, I think. Little Annie showed remarkable talent."

I watched Mrs. Pots speak, afraid of what she was going to say next. I knew for a fact that she lived alone in town, so I suspected this story couldn't end very well.

"She died about twenty years ago," she continued. "Freak accident; no one could have prevented it. She and her aunt Twila were both killed in an accident. Tore me and Bill apart, too. He's living down in Florida with his family. Haven't spoken in some years, now."

"I'm so sorry, Mrs. Pots." I had no idea. My heart was breaking for the poor woman. I also felt rather terrible, as I've considered her a close friend since moving to Brimstone Bay, and not once did I think to ask whether she had a family at one point. I just assumed she had always lived alone, devoting her life to that little bakery.

"Oh, it's fine, dear," she said. "Happened so long ago. I'm just so happy to have you girls so I can feel the joys of being surrounded by magic again." She sighed deeply, then got lost, gazing into the fire.

We all lost ourselves as well, entranced by the flames coming from the hot fire in front of us.

"Let's have some fun, shall we?" Mrs. Brody said in attempt to lighten the mood. She flicked her wrist before the fire, and the flames transformed into a myriad of wondrous shapes, all dancing and folding into one another.

Bailey then took over the show from Mrs. Brody, changing the flames from unnamed shapes to cats, chasing each other around the coals. We all laughed as one of the cats bit down on the other cat's tail. I swear I could almost hear the hissing sound come from the shape of the cat in the fire.

Mrs. Pots was beaming at the fire, absolutely enthralled with the beauty of the magic happening before her. She began humming a tune and clapping her hands, creating a musical rhythm as the background to the cats performing in the fire.

"What are you girls dressing up as tomorrow night?" Mrs. Brody asked us as Bailey refilled her mug with cider.

"I was thinking of going as a witch," I laughed. "Seems fitting."

Mrs. Brody laughed at that. "Oh, how clever."

"What about you?"

"Oh, it's a secret, dear. You'll see tomorrow night."

"How about you, Mrs. Pots?" Rory asked.

"Nothing fancy, I'm afraid," she answered, taking a break from her melody. "I'll be serving cakes and goodies all night, I don't want to get a costume all dirty. I was thinking of going as a baker, which seems to go along with River's highly original costume theme."

"Oh, come on, that's cheating," I laughed. "You wear baker's clothes all day at the bakery. That's nothing new! It's not like I go around wearing robes and a witch hat."

Mrs. Pots shrugged. "Well, if you come up with a better idea before tomorrow, let me know. What about the rest of you girls?"

Rory, Bailey, and Jane began to giggle.

"It's a secret," Jane said. "You'll all see tomorrow."

I raised my eyebrow at them, curious as to what devious plan they had cooked up this time.

"Give us a hint," I said.

"Nope," Bailey said simply, crossing her arms. "You'll have to wait until tomorrow."

CHAPTER FOUR

THE HOUSE HAD A BUZZING ELECTRIC ENERGY ABOUT it when I woke up the next day.

I could already hear the sound of feet shuffling from the floor above me, and knew my housemates were awake. I reached over for my phone on my bedside table and groaned when I saw that it was only 6 am. I was no stranger to waking up early, and often loved to go for runs first thing in the morning as the sun came up, but it was nearing winter and it was dark outside, and my room was drafty and I wanted nothing more than to stay in bed all day curled up under my comforters.

I rolled over and pressed one of my pillows over my face to try and muffle the sounds of the morning so I could get at least another hour or two of sleep.

That dream was short lived when I heard a loud meow in my ear and felt a paw prod at my neck.

I sighed and threw off the pillow to be met by three little fuzzy faces looking down at me.

"Hey guys," I said through a loud yawn. Big fat momma cat came up and plunked herself down on my chest, pinning me to my bed. "Thanks, Momma. Now I have an excuse to stay in bed." She closed her eyes and purred as I scratched her behind her ear.

Soot and the new little kitten, Agnes, curled up together next to me, and I closed my eyes to try and fall back asleep. Only I could feel my eyes growing itchy, and a sudden sneeze spooked the cats off my bed and pulled me out of my groggy state.

I sighed and stretched, then grudgingly pushed myself out of bed to get started on the day.

There would be last minute preparations to help with for the party tonight, so I grabbed a towel from the pile in the corner of my room and went to have a shower.

Mrs. Brody had me working to the bone all morning, setting up tables and putting out more decorations. She had an entire room full of stuff that had to be brought down to the beach, which was definitely a task in itself, given the fact that there were about one hundred stairs between our backyard and the beach down below.

The day went by really fast, and I was actually feeling quite excited for the party. It would be nice to have an excuse to hang out with other people in the town for once.

The band had arrived and was setting up in the backyard when I decided to head back inside to get ready and put my costume on. Luckily, my costume consisted of a hat and a cloak, so, it wouldn't really take any time at all.

The girls, on the other hand, had been hidden away in their rooms for hours, working on their secret costumes. I had no idea what they were up to, but I could bet it would be amazing.

It sounded like there were bombs going off upstairs. Loud crashes and bangs followed by loud giggling came from the floor above me as I got changed. I resisted the urge to go upstairs and see what they were up to, but curiosity was nearly getting the better of me.

"What do you think they're up to?" I asked Soot as he jumped up on my bed beside me. He flopped over onto his back for some much overdue belly scratches. The poor cat had missed being the center of attention since Agnes and Momma turned up. He purred loudly as I scratched.

Another loud clang came from the floor above me and I rolled my eyes, trying to ignore them.

I rummaged through my makeup bag and realized I really didn't have any proper costume makeup. My kit consisted of mascara and lip balm - not really Halloween appropriate. This was the one day per year you could really go all out with your makeup and wardrobe, and I definitely needed more than what I had to take full advantage.

Between Rory and Bailey, those girls had every type of makeup under the sun, and after a few more loud bangs came from above me, I decided to see what they could do to help. Climbing up on my bedside table, I knocked my fist a few times against the ceiling. "Hey, do you guys have any makeup I could borrow?" I called up through the floor.

The room upstairs went quiet for a minute, then a small glittery makeup bag with the letter B appeared on my bed. "Thanks, Bailey!"

The loud noises resumed upstairs, and I could only imagine what sort of mess they were creating.

Poking through Bailey's makeup bag, I noticed there was nothing sophisticated about its contents. I dumped the contents onto my bed and saw purple glitter eye shadows and bright pink lipsticks. I sighed to myself, then picked up a sparkled black eyeliner pen and began carefully painting it across my lids.

After twenty strenuous minutes of applying makeup, I took a step back and looked at myself in the mirror. I hardly recognized the girl looking back at me. Sweeping, glittery cat eyes and glossy red lips were startling, but, for one night, what the hell.

I grabbed my witch's hat that I bought at a pop-up Halloween shop in town and placed it upon my head. Well, I definitely looked the part, now. I couldn't help but laugh at myself.

Music sounded through my window as the band began to play.

"I guess that's my cue," I said to the cats, who were watching me intently as I had attempted to do my makeup. I swung the black cloak over my shoulders and went to join Mrs. Brody in the backyard to greet the guests.

Streams of people were already arriving, and the festival was in full swing. Mrs. Brody had hung a large banner between two trees near the rear of the yard that said "Hallows' Bay" on it. The lettering flickered and glowed in the moonlight, and I guessed Mrs. Brody wouldn't be holding back on her magical tricks tonight.

I poured myself a mug of hot cider, then went to go chat with Mrs. Pots, who was busying herself behind the food table, setting out her last minute cakes and treats.

"Nice spread," I said. I reached for a small orange-colored cookie and took a bite. "This is amazing. What is it?" The cookie melted in my mouth like butter.

"A new creation," Mrs. Pots said cheerfully. "Pumpkin butter cookies. My own recipe."

"Well, they're amazing," I said as I grabbed another.

"Thank you, dear. What lovely makeup you have on tonight."

"I can say the same to you," I said. Mrs. Pots had painted her face white with smudged black around her eyes. "What exactly are you?"

"A dead baker," she said as she posed. "Can't you tell?"

"You look great."

"Where are the other girls?" Mrs. Pots asked, standing on her toes to try and see over the growing crowd.

I shook my head. "They're still inside getting ready. They've been obsessing over their secret costumes since yesterday morning."

"I bet we're in for a treat, then," Mrs. Pots said as she turned to her task of setting out the rest of the treats.

Mrs. Pots continued to work as I went to find Mrs. Brody to see if she needed help with anything. The crowd was growing at an alarming rate, and it seemed nearly the whole town had shown up. The rear yard was packed, and when I walked out to the bluff and looked down at the bay below, a large crowd had grown there, too.

I looked around for familiar faces, but, with everyone in costume, it was difficult to tell who was who. After a few minutes of searching, a voice came calling out from the crowd behind me. "River! River, over here!"

I turned to see Grace waving to me over the crowd. Trey was with her, and I went over to join them. Grace gave me a big hug, and then stepped back and posed for me. "How do I look?"

"You both look fantastic," I said as I admired their costumes. Both were dressed up as sort of Frankenstein zombies. Grace had painted their faces to look like they were stitched up, and they wore torn clothes with fake blood. They really did look awesome.

"Thanks. Nice witch costume." She winked at me, then reached for my hand. "Come, let's get some drinks. Yours looks empty."

Grace pulled me towards the nearest drink table and poured us all some punch. "Not a bad party for such a little town."

I shrugged. "Brimstone Bay isn't that bad. I had reservations about moving to a small town after living in New York, but I kind of like it here."

Grace shook her head dramatically and made a slashing motion along her neck with her finger. "Couldn't do it myself. Back to the big city for us, soon. Once the restaurant gets off the ground, we'll go back where we're needed, running the main place in New York."

I glanced at Trey who was staring down at his feet.

"And what do you think about that?" I asked him, nudging him with my elbow.

He shrugged. "I like it here. It's quiet."

I laughed. "Oh, not as quiet as you might think."

I turned to look behind us when I heard my name being called again. Mayor Scott and Jordan were walking up to us, and I nearly doubled over I was laughing so hard.

"What?" Jordan asked as they came up to us.

I tried my best to regain my composure, but it was just too much. Jordan was dressed as a vampire, which, with his striking ice blue eyes, looked really quite sexy, but Mayor Scott was dressed up as a werewolf.

"Nice costumes," I said to them. I couldn't get over the Mayor's costume. He was a werewolf, after all. But I was likely the only one in town who knew the truth about what he was. I couldn't decide if it was brave, hilarious, or simply stupid of him to come dressed like that. A bit of column a, but of column b, I guessed.

"Thanks," Jordan said. "You look great." He pulled me in for a one-armed hug. I did my best not to swoon.

"Drinks?" I asked, hoping that the blush I could feel growing on my cheeks wasn't noticeable in the dark. The sun had set, and the decorations were in their full glory. The candles cast a warm glow over the entire yard and the firelight flickered against the trees. It was shaping up to be a really great night.

"Where are your friends?" Grace asked.

"Still getting ready, I guess," I said. "They've been working on their costumes all day. Hope they come out soon."

As if on cue, two of my housemates came walking out of the house towards us.

"Oh. My. God." I fell to my knees I was laughing so hard. "You guys, what are you doing!"

Jane and Rory were dressed as Soot and Agnes, my two cats.

"We're your cats," Rory said.

"The cats to your witch," Jane winked at me.

Rory was wearing a skin-tight black and white body suit with cute fuzzy cat ears and whiskers drawn on her cheeks, obviously dressed as the little kitten, Agnes. She looked like she should be on a stage at a show. She looked remarkable.

Jane was dressed as soot, and was wearing a sophisticated gray business suit with a bow tie and ears.

I wiped the tears from my eyes as I shook my head. "You guys are hilarious. Where's Bailey?" I thought it was a safe bet to guess who Bailey was dressed up as, but I had to see it for myself.

"She's coming. She's having a hard time navigating the stairs." Rory laughed.

"Huh?" I asked.

"Here she comes," Jane said.

I turned to look at the house and saw a giant

fuzzy white figure come waddling out to the backyard.

"You're kidding me," I said. "How did you guys even make that?"

"It took all day and some serious craftiness," Rory laughed.

Bailey was wearing a full head-to-toe white fur suit, complete with footies and a fuzzy cat head. They had cut holes for the eyes for her to see through, but, apart from that, her body was completely covered. She looked absolutely ridiculous.

"Hey Momma," I said as she made her way clumsily towards us.

She took off the giant cat head and wiped sweat from her brow. "It's freaking hot in here."

We all laughed, and I pulled her in for a hug. "Ouu, fuzzy," I said into her suit.

She laughed. "It seemed like a really great idea at the time. But now, not so sure."

"At least, you won't need a jacket," I suggested.

"Oh, you guys, I need to take a photo of this." Grace pulled out her phone from her purse and waited for us all to pose together—the witch and her three cats.

Grace excitedly snapped a bunch of photos, then promised to send them to us online. I still couldn't get over the girls' costumes. Considering we just got the two new cats yesterday morning, it's no wonder they had spent so much time cooped up in their rooms making the costumes. I had no idea how they managed to make all three of those things in less than two days.

"I'm starved," Grace said. "What's there to eat around here?"

"Mrs. Pots catered the party," I answered. "Have you guys met her yet? She runs the bakery in town."

"Oh, we've met her. The bakery's right across from the restaurant," Grace said wryly. "Claims to have the best cakes in town. We'll see about that."

"Be nice," I said. "That bakery has been here for over twenty years. Don't go all big city on her."

Grace rolled her eyes. "I'm always nice."

I smirked. Sure, she was.

We all walked over to Mrs. Pots' food table to load up on snacks.

"Hi, Mrs. Pots," Grace smiled. "Beautiful table you've got here." She reached for one of the small pumpkin butter cookies and took a bite.

"Hello, Grace. Nice to see you," Mrs. Pots feigned a smile, but it was hardly believable.

"Wow, these are good," Grace said through a crumbling bite. "Reminds me of these darling little cakes Trey makes. You should try them. You'd go nuts over them!"

"I'll keep it in mind," Mrs. Pots answered, then turned her back to us as she rummaged through her bag behind the table.

You've gotta hand it to the woman, at least she's making an effort to be somewhat friendly. I don't know how I would handle having someone swoop into my town and threaten my business.

Mrs. Brody called from the other side of the yard, and I left poor Mrs. Pots alone with Grace and Trey as the girls and I went to help Mrs. Brody with whatever it was she had planned. Trey was a really friendly guy, and I could hear him strike up a conversation with Mrs. Pots about her favorite ingredients as I walked away. I hoped they all learned to get along, as it's never a good idea to piss off the competition. Besides, a little friendly competition never hurt anyone, right?

"We're going to get the fire ceremony set up, can you girls gather all the guests?" Mrs. Brody asked. "I've just about got it set up now."

Mrs. Brody had set up a circle of logs around the fire, and had positioned various bags and metal containers on the ground as well. Peeking inside the nearest bag, I saw some sort of colorful dust. Unsure what the contents of the bags were, I felt it was better to just let her unveil her mystery rather than pry.

I went around the yard, gathering the guests to the bonfire. There had to be at least a couple hundred people, and not everyone would be able to see the fire, but Mrs. Brody assured me that wouldn't be an issue, so I gathered the rest of the crowd anyway.

The band finished playing their song, and, on Mrs. Brody's cue, began playing some eerie background music to set the mood. The crowd hushed in anticipation. I didn't know what was coming, but the rest of the guests seemed to. I was probably the only one here who hadn't been to one of these parties before, I guessed.

Mrs. Brody coughed to clear her throat. "We are gathered in on Hallows' Eve to celebrate the spirits at Hallows' Bay."

The crowd clapped as she spoke, and cheered at the mention of Hallows' Bay. It was a cute nickname, I'll give them that.

"With light, there is dark, and in dark, we get light," she announced dramatically as she tossed a handful of the colorful dust in the fire.

The crowd let out cheers of awe as the fire erupted into a magical show of colors and shapes, soaring high above the rooftops into the sky above. The forms erupted in the sky into orange jack-o-lanterns, white ghosts, and red stars. The demonstration was spectacular, and I could see why everyone spoke so highly of the party. Mrs. Brody's light show beat any fireworks I'd ever seen in the big city.

"We hide behind our costumes, but allow our true souls to shine through on this celebrated night," she continued. "Ghouls, witches, vampires—who are we to know what is real and what is show?"

She tossed another handful of dust on the fire and it erupted into a red flaming cat who pounced around the treetops, chasing small sparkling bats that flew from the fire before it.

I cheered as the cat appeared and my housemates meowed. I still couldn't get over their costumes.

As the cat and bats disappeared, the roaring fire died down slightly, and a thick white smoke began to spread around our feet. The crowd hushed again.

As the flames lowered, I could see Jordan on the other side of the bonfire. He winked at me as he caught my eye, and I hoped the red glow from the fire masked the redness in my cheeks. I cursed myself for blushing. I was a grown woman, yet a boy still made me blush. How embarrassing. I smiled back at him through the flames as Mrs. Brody tossed another handful of dust on the fire.

This time the fire began to roil, as if the flames were smoke in a cauldron.

"We gather this night to celebrate the living, to celebrate the dead, and to celebrate those caught in between."

The atmosphere had grown momentarily sombre as the hushed crowd remembered their lost loved ones.

"Tonight, the dead celebrate among us."

Suddenly, a loud, high-pitched scream erupted

from behind the crowd. "He's dead," the voice shrieked.

I thought at first it was part of the show, but when Mrs. Brody quieted the flames and the crowd began to chatter, I knew it wasn't part of the plan.

"Help, somebody! He's dead!"

I ran towards the voice that I recognized as Grace's. The crowd parted and I bolted forward towards the body lying on the ground in front of Mrs. Pots' treat table.

I looked down into Trey's face, his skin was stark white and his eyes empty.

CHAPTER FIVE

GRACE COLLAPSED IN A BALL ON THE GROUND NEXT to Trey, sobbing into her hands as the crowd pressed forward.

"Let me through," Mayor Scott pushed through the crowd, accompanied by Jordan. Jordan immediately threw himself on the ground next to Trey and began CPR.

I fumbled for my phone and called for an ambulance. I was through to 911 immediately, and they said an ambulance was on the way. I pressed my hand up against my other ear to block out the growing noise of the crowd as I tried my best to answer the questions the person on the phone line was asking me.

I glanced around for Sheriff Reese, but couldn't spot him in the crowd. Not a good night for him to skip out on a party.

"Get back, everyone," Mayor Scott shouted at the pressing crowd. "Clear some room. Let Officer O'Riley work."

"Not an officer anymore," Jordan said as he worked on Trey's chest. I watched, frozen in place as he gave mouth to mouth to his friend.

"Is there anything I can do?" I asked. I continued to hold the phone up to my ear, as the attendant asked me to stay on the line.

The Mayor succeeded in getting the crowd to move back, and a large portion of the guests were leaving. I silently thanked him. He was getting to be really good in situations like this. An unfortunate thing to be good at, but helpful nonetheless.

For the next few, long minutes, we all watched Jordan work on the lifeless body on the ground.

I moved to sit next to Grace and put my arm around her shoulder as her sobbing quieted to silent heaves. I stroked her back, knowing full well that nothing I did or said could make her feel any better in this situation.

I glanced up at the people surrounding us as it felt like time was standing still.

Mrs. Brody was busy shooing the rest of the guests away, and the girls were looking down in horror. Mrs. Pots was standing frozen behind her table with her eyes wide and her hands pressed over her mouth. She looked pale, as if she would pass out any second. I caught Bailey's eye and motioned towards Mrs. Pots with my eyes. She understood, and moved to stand next to Mrs. Pots, wrapping her arms around her shoulders. It was quite the sight, given the massive white fuzzy cat costume she was wearing. But Mrs. Pots welcomed the affection, and leaned her plump face on Bailey's furry shoulder.

Jordan eventually stopped his attempt at resuscitating Trey, and sat back on his feet. He was breathing heavily and shaking his head.

"NO!" Grace cried out, throwing her body over Trey's. "He's not dead. Please, no! He can't be dead."

She stroked the hair off her husband's white face, her tears falling onto his forehead. He had orange cookie crumbs over his shirt and at the corners of his mouth, and she wiped them away dutifully.

"Did you see him choke?" Jordan asked Grace, barely holding back the tremble in his voice.

She shook her head. "I don't know. I wasn't watching. He just fell." She choked back sobs as she spoke, speaking each word slowly.

Jordan ran his hands through his hair, staring down at his friend as he shook his head. "I don't understand."

The ambulance pulled up along the side of the house and cast red and blue lights over the scene.

I saw Sheriff Reese arrive with the paramedics,

and they were pulling a gurney from the back of the vehicle.

I turned my attention back to the body, and bent down next to Jordan as I noticed something strange about Trey's eyes.

"What's that?" I asked, squinting closer at the skin around his eyes.

Jordan followed my gaze and inspected the strange markings.

Streams of light blue were spreading like little lightning forks from the corners of his eyes under the skin. After a moment, the same began forming at the corners of his mouth.

"I've never seen anything like that before," Jordan said.

"Could he have been poisoned?" I asked. Trey's face was taking on a strange mask-like quality. It was as if someone had painted a pattern under his skin.

"P..p..poisoned?" Grace made out, her eyes growing wider.

She immediately jumped up and pointed at Mrs. Pots. "HER! It was her, I know it was. I saw her give Trey that cookie. She killed him! I saw her!"

Everyone grew quiet at the accusation, and I stared back and forth between Grace and Mrs. Pots. Mrs. Pots seemed to still be in shock, and I'm not sure she even noticed Grace's accusation.

"That's not possible, Grace," I said, trying to

sound level-headed. "Don't be ridiculous. This was an accident. He choked, end of story."

Grace shook her head and looked livid. "No. I knew from the moment we first met her that she wanted us gone. The way she looked at us when we first moved in across the street, I knew she had darkness within her."

"Grace, dear," Mrs. Brody said, placing a hand on Grace's shoulder. "Don't say things we can't take back. We all know Mrs. Pots very well in this town. She's not capable of hurting a fly."

"NO!" Grace shouted again, stepping towards Mrs. Pots with her hand outstretched. "I saw her, just now. She was the one who poisoned him. I know it. I saw it!"

I picked up a few cookie crumbs from the ground next to Trey's body, and held them up to Grace. "Grace, it was an accident. A freak accident. I'm so sorry, Grace. Trey choked."

I then immediately withdrew my hand from the air and let the crumbs fall to the ground. My skin that had touched the cookie crumbs began to burn. "What the…" I began, staring down at the pieces of cookie that I had just dropped.

"Let me see that," Mrs. Brody said. She bent over and picked up the pieces I had just dropped, then waved her other hand over it and cast a quiet spell.

The pieces of cookie began to smoke, and then

disintegrated into a pile of ash in her hand. We all stared at the small pile of gray ash she held.

"What does that mean?" Rory asked, stepping forward.

Mrs. Brody looked up at each of us in turn. "Magic."

I stared at her incredulously. "Magic? What do you mean?"

"Dark magic," she corrected. "This cookie was tainted with dark magic."

"I knew it!" Grace cried. "You murdered my husband!" She collapsed on the ground again and sobbed into her hands.

The few remaining people in the crowd moved aside as the paramedics arrived with the gurney, and worked together with Jordan and Mayor Scott to lift Trey's body onto the table.

Sheriff Reese came up to us and took in the scene. "What happened?" he asked.

Mayor Scott explained the situation to him, carefully explaining how Trey had choked on a cookie and we were unable to resuscitate him.

"He was murdered!" Grace shouted hysterically to the Sheriff. "The baker woman. I saw her. She gave him a poisoned cookie."

Sheriff Reese looked to Mrs. Pots who was still standing frozen in place, her hands pressed firmly over her mouth. Bailey pulled her tighter into a hug, holding her tight.

"Is this true?" he asked.

"Of course, not," Mrs. Brody spat at him. "Don't be absurd. You know Mrs. Pots is not capable of any such thing."

The Sheriff nodded. "Indeed," he whispered quietly to himself. He rubbed his chin as he looked back and forth between Mrs. Brody, Grace, and the place on the ground where Trey had fallen.

"She did," Grace sobbed. "I saw her. She murdered him because she thinks we were going to put her out of business."

"These are very serious accusations," Sheriff Reese said plainly to her. He then turned to the rest of us and asked, "Did any of you see this?"

I shook my head. "He choked."

"His face suggests differently," he said to me.

"You murdered my husband," Grace repeated, her face pressed into her hands as she rolled onto her side on the ground.

Mrs. Brody sat next to her and stroked her hair, then looked up at the Sheriff. "The cookie was poisoned. This we know."

Sheriff Reese nodded. "That I believe." He looked to Mrs. Pots and his eyes grew sad.

"I'm so sorry, Nancy," he said slowly as he made his way to join Mrs. Pots on the other side of the table. "I'm going to have to take you in. Protocol, and all that."

She stared at him and nodded her head slowly.

Poor woman seemed too in shock to really understand what was going on.

"Don't be ridiculous, Sheriff," I said. "Mrs. Pots had nothing to do with this."

"If she did in fact give him the poisoned cookie, that makes her a suspect." Then, after seeing my angry eyes glaring at him, he added, "I have to do something."

I shook my head at him, then stood and went to join Bailey in holding Mrs. Pots.

"He called for backup on his walkie-talkie. "This table is evidence. Please, everyone, stand back. The party is over."

"I'm coming with you," I said to Mrs. Pots.

"We are all coming with you," Bailey added.

I saw Jane, Rory, and Mrs. Brody all nod in agreement.

"Don't worry, we'll figure this out," I said to Mrs. Pots as I stroked her arm. I could feel her shaking.

"No," Mayor Scott said. "There has to be an explanation." He had known Mrs. Pots since he was a kid, and, just like the rest of us, couldn't believe she had anything to do with this.

Sheriff Reese tilted Mrs. Pots' chin up to make eye contact with her when she continued to stare down at her feet. "Did you give him that cookie?"

She stared back at him, then nodded.

Sheriff Reese sighed, then brought out his hand

cuffs and turned the poor small woman around and cuffed her hands behind her back.

I kept looking back and forth between Grace and Mrs. Pots, not having any clue what to do or say.

"Don't worry," I said finally, unsure who I was really speaking to.

Grace stared up at us incredulously, her lips pursed in a tight line and her eyes looking angrier than I'd ever seen them. "Why are you standing by her?" she asked. "She murdered my husband."

I looked down at Grace and shook my head. "I don't believe that. There must be an explanation. There's absolutely no way Mrs. Pots is responsible for this. Please, believe me."

Grace glared daggers at me, then snapped, "You always were a pathetic one." She then stood up and turned to follow the paramedics back to the ambulance. The lights had been turned off and the crew didn't seem to be in a rush. Why would they be, as the guy was already dead and there was nothing they could do about it.

We all watched as Grace got into the ambulance with the paramedics, and then they drove off, leaving the rest of us standing in the rear yard in silence.

CHAPTER SIX

"UNTIL WE HAVE MORE INFORMATION, WE'RE GOING to treat this as a crime scene," Sheriff Reese told us. "Mrs. Brody, please make sure the rest of the guests clear the yard. I'll ask a few of my men to stay behind to keep an eye on things."

He waved his hand at the direction of the table. "Can you girls please take a look at the food and let me know if you find anything... unnatural, okay? I'll expect a full report in the morning."

"We're going with Mrs. Pots." I crossed my arms stubbornly and stared Sheriff Reese in the eye.

He let out a loud sigh, but kept his silence.

Mrs. Pots slowly pushed herself back up and flattened out her apron. "No, dear, you'll do no such thing."

"Don't be absurd," Bailey said. "We're coming with you. We all know it wasn't you, Mrs. Pots."

Mrs. Pots shook her head. "It was my cookie. I gave him that cookie. He died because of something I gave him." She then turned to Sheriff Reese. "I'll cooperate fully. Take me in."

We all stared at her in shock. My mouth fell agape, and I couldn't formulate what to even say to her.

Finally, I settled on something dumb, as per usual. "But, no." I looked back and forth between Sheriff Reese and Mrs. Pots, expecting either to say something along the lines of "Just kidding" or "Happy October Fool's Day" or whatever.

When neither said anything, and Sheriff Reese began leading Mrs. Pots back to his car, I felt completely and utterly deflated.

"Mrs. Brody, the guests?" the Sheriff reminded her. "Please, see to it that this place gets cleared out and that the treats are examined thoroughly. The boys will take some samples, but given the funny nature of what seems to be going on here, I'd like to hear firsthand from you what you think happened."

Mrs. Brody nodded dutifully to the young Sheriff Reese.

"And don't you think for one second that any of you are off the hook," he added. "I expect you all in my office first thing tomorrow morning for questioning. If any funny business is going on, I better not be able to trace it back to you lot."

With that he left, and Mrs. Pots followed with her head hung low.

Mayor Scott walked up to us and rubbed his forehead, a stress habit that he had adopted earlier that month, I noticed. "We'll follow Reese to the precinct. Call me if you find anything, okay? Promise you won't do anything... out of the ordinary." He eyed me when he said those last words.

I nodded slowly to him, then watched him and Jordan follow Sheriff Reese to his car.

"I don't understand," I finally managed. "I just... I just don't understand."

"Neither do any of us, dear," Mrs. Brody said. She moved to stand beside me and then placed one hand on my shoulder. I could feel a tear trickling down my cheek.

"Well, there's nothing we can do to help her now," Rory said. "So, we might as well do as he says and take a good look at the crime scene."

"It's not a crime scene," I said stubbornly. "We all know Mrs. Pots isn't capable of murder. Even accidental murder."

Rory nodded to me. "I know."

"And there's no way she would have found that kind of dark magic to put in a cookie," I continued. "We're the only witches she knows in town, and none of us conjured anything up like that. Right?" I looked back and forth between my housemates and

Mrs. Brody. They all nodded in agreement. Thank the spirits. I let out a loud breath I didn't know I was holding.

It felt weird discussing something as serious as murder with a tiny little pink-haired witch and three adult women dressed as cats. Given our track record, though, I really shouldn't have been surprised.

"I'll go about sending the rest of the lingerers home," Mrs. Brody said as she made her way back around the table to join the rest of the guests.

Two officers had arrived and were cordoning off the dessert table and surrounding area with police tape.

"Is that absolutely necessary?" I asked. "It's our backyard. No one else will be coming around once we get the guests to leave."

One of the officers, I knew him as Jack, shrugged. "Protocol, miss." Jack went about collecting some crumbs from the ground as evidence and tucked the little clear bag away in his jacket pocket.

I sighed. "Yeah, okay. Sure."

I sat down on the grass and rubbed my temples, trying to think. There was absolutely no way Mrs. Brody could have been involved, of that much I was sure. It's just a matter of proving it. How we were going to do that with a firsthand witness speaking against us, I had no idea.

"Do you think Grace will be okay?" Bailey asked me quietly as she joined me on the ground.

I shook my head. "Doubt it. How would you feel if the man you just married died?"

Bailey looked down at her feet. "I can't even imagine. The poor girl."

"At least, she still has the business," Jane offered, joining us on the ground as well. "Hopefully, that keeps her distracted through this. When my grandmother died two years ago, it was during the middle of exams. It made writing the exams more difficult, but the distraction really helped me through it."

"Yeah, I hope you're right," I said. I made a mental note to call Emily in the morning.

After a few minutes, Mrs. Brody joined us and let us know the guests had all left.

Rory sighed and looked around the yard. "It's such a shame. The party was just getting started. It's not even midnight yet."

"Why does this always seem to happen to us?" I asked. "First, the Shadow Festival, now this."

Mrs. Brody crossed her arms and gave me a stern look. "This has nothing to do with any of us. It's nothing more than an unfortunate event at an unfortunate time."

"I guess," I agreed.

"Now, let's get this thing figured out before poor Mrs. Pots rots away in jail, shall we?" Mrs. Brody moved to the other side of the dessert table and began inspecting the treats. The rest of us joined her, and we spent the next hour or so carefully going over every piece of food.

"Well, there's definitely nothing wrong with any of the other food," Mrs. Brody announced after a thorough inspection.

"The entire table is fine," Bailey agreed. She waved her hands once more over the entirety of the table, and then nodded. "Definitely no traces of magic. None whatsoever."

"So, it's just the one cookie, then?" I began poking through Mrs. Pots' bags and containers under the table. "I'm not sensing any traces of magic in any of her things. Don't you think at least a small trace would show up where the cookie was stored?"

"Absolutely," Mrs. Brody said. "Unless she conjured the magic on the spot, but we all know she's not capable of that."

I laughed. "She's not a witch. Of course, she's not capable of that."

"Not only that," Rory added. "She's the kindest woman in town. Even if she did have the ability, she still wouldn't have been capable of that sort of magic."

We all nodded in agreement.

"So, now what?" I asked.

"We find as many crumbs as we can, and try and

learn as much as we can about the magic that killed Trey," Bailey answered.

We all set about searching the grass for any remaining crumbs. It was the middle of the night, so it was easier said than done. Mrs. Brody had waved over some of the surrounding lights, but, between the four of us crawling around on the ground and the inconsistent flicker of the candle light, our shadows made the task even more difficult.

"Nice, look what I found," Jane said after a few long minutes of searching. She waved a large chunk of orange cookie in front of us. "Must have rolled under the table."

"Awesome. Great work," I told her.

Mrs. Brody waved her hand over the treat and a dark aura began to glow around it. "That's the same cookie, alright. Be careful."

I reached for a container under the table and handed it to Jane, who carefully placed the cookie inside.

"Shall we go in where there's more light?" Rory suggested.

I sighed. "Yeah, I guess so." I took in the scene of the decorated yard one last time. "It really does look amazing out here." Thick white smoke still clung to the base of the trees that surrounded the yard, glowing a warm yellow from the surrounding lanterns and other lit decorations. It was gloriously spooky.

We all began to head into the house when Mrs. Brody's watch alarm went off.

"Oh, will you look at that," she said as she inspected the large gaudy watch around her wrist. "It's midnight."

"Happy midnight," I said unenthusiastically.

Bailey laughed at me. "That's the spirit." She rolled her eyes.

We all looked up at the moon, which was nearly full and glowing a warm orange. The sky was quite cloudy and we couldn't see the stars, but the glow from the moon illuminated the surroundings all on its own.

"Come on, let's go," Mrs. Brody said as she led the way back to the house. I hung back, not quite wanting to give up on the magic of the night just yet.

I took in a deep breath of the cool autumn air, soaking in all the positive energy the moon gave off. I could feel myself grow calmer by the second. I then shivered, realizing the strange effect the moon just had on me. I grew up a witch, so I knew we had a strong relationship with nature, but I'd never really felt it this intensely before. Growing up near New York City, we really didn't have access to this much unspoiled nature.

I sighed, then reluctantly followed the rest of the girls and Mrs. Brody inside. At least, I felt invigorated, and felt like I could take on just about anything right then. Thank the spirits, as I had a feeling the next few days were going to be long ones.

Everyone was clustered around the kitchen table when I arrived. The container with the remaining cookie sat at the center of the table, and I noticed three particularly curious looking cats had joined the party. The real cats, not the ridiculous costumed ones that were my housemates.

"Okay," I laughed as I joined them at the table. "Six is just way too many cats. You guys are going to have to do something about this."

Bailey giggled and picked up Momma cat and placed her on her lap. Between Bailey's massive furry suit and the fat cat's white fur, you could hardly tell where one ended and the other began.

Rory reached for little Agnes, who flopped on her back on the table in front of her, demanding attention. Soot hopped up on Jane's lap and began pawing at her bow tie.

"It's as if they know," I said, looking incredulously at the scene in front of me. "These cats never cease to amaze me."

"They're smarter than you think," Rory said as she tickled little Agnes' belly on the table.

I shook my head, not really believing the ridiculousness of what was going on around me.

"How lovely," Mrs. Brody said. "A witch, her bitches, and their queens."

I stared at her for a second, processing what she

had just said, then immediately lost myself in a fit of giggles. Everyone else in the room laughed as well, and some of the tension that had built up in the room dissipated immediately.

Mrs. Brody got up to make some tea, and we all settled down after a few good moments of much needed laugher to get down to business.

"Okay, so what do we know?" I asked, pulling the container with the cookie towards me to inspect it closer.

"Well," Bailey said. "We know there's magic in the cookie."

"Dark magic," Jane corrected.

"Dark magic," Bailey repeated. "And we know Trey ate part of the cookie, then died."

We all sat in silence for a moment, the recollection of what had happened loomed over our heads like dark clouds.

I shook my head, trying my best to clear my mind so I could think. "But why? Is there any way this could have been an accident?"

"Could have just been a coincidence," Rory said. "Maybe the cookie wasn't meant for him? Or maybe, just maybe, it was a spell gone wrong." She eyed Mrs. Brody.

"Maybe the person who spelled the cookie meant for it to do something else," Jane said, following Bailey's train of thought.

Mrs. Brody joined us at the table with a tray of

teacups and a pot of steaming chai tea. "I highly doubt that." She pulled the container towards her, and bent close to examine the cookie. "I haven't seen magic like this in a long time. Whoever conjured the spell must have been very powerful. This was deliberate, there's no doubt about that.

I sighed. "Okay, so we've established that. What we really need to find out now was whether it was actually intended for Trey, and who was the one who cast the spell?"

Bailey shook her head. "I didn't sense any powerful magic at the party. Nothing apart from the typical buzz you get from people who have diluted magic in them from family heritage. If there was another powerful witch here, we would have sensed it."

"You're right," I said. I then slumped back into my chair and squeezed my eyes shut in concentration. "Then how did it get into Mrs. Pots' possession? Who brought it here?"

"Can we put a tracking spell on it?" Rory asked. "Maybe it can lead us to the person who made the magic."

I sat bolt upright as if a new surge of energy coursed through my veins. "Of course! That's a brilliant idea. It could lead us right to them."

I looked over to Mrs. Brody who looked skeptical.

"What is it?" I asked. "Don't you think we can do it?"

She paused a moment, then answered. "Well, for a tracking spell to work correctly we need an item that belongs to the person."

I shrugged. "Easy. The cookie."

Mrs. Brody shook her head. "No, dear, that belongs to Mrs. Pots. I doubt anyone replicated a cookie for their own use."

I eyed the cookie then slumped back down into my chair. "Right."

After a few long silent minutes of everyone staring at the remnants of the orange cookie on the table, I decided it was at least worth a shot.

"We don't have any other options," I said. "We might as well try and see if we can find any sort of trace, however small, of where the magic itself came from."

"We could test the magic's DNA," Bailey offered.

I blinked. "What now?"

Bailey laughed. "Every magic user has their own unique magical DNA. Think of it sort of like a fingerprint."

I shook my head at the girl. "You really are amazing, you know that?"

She blushed, then shrugged. "Just something I learned somewhere…" she trailed off.

"How do we test it?" Jane asked.

Bailey shook her head. "I don't know, exactly. I imagine it would be similar to a tracking spell. I've never done it before."

"Any idea where we can learn how?" Jane asked.

"No idea," Bailey answered. "Nowhere around here, at least."

"Worth a shot," I said. "It's our only option. Why don't we attempt a tracking spell, only instead of focusing on the owner of the object, we focus on the owner of the magic."

Mrs. Brody nodded along silently. "Yes, that could work." She then stood up and moved toward the large cabinet in the kitchen and rummaged through her many odd jars and containers.

She returned with an armful of items, including various spices, grinding tools, and bowls.

I watched intently as she set about placing the items in a pattern in front of her. I didn't have an affinity for this kind of spell, so I let the others work their magic, so to speak. It did seem old school though, and I loved it. I guess being a modern witch really removed you from the old classic witch stuff. I felt like I was in some sort of Halloween movie. Fitting, really.

"Frog's weed?" Bailey asked as Mrs. Brody took out a clump of dried, brown hay-like twigs.

Mrs. Brody nodded. "I thought it would be a nice touch. Might make the link between the magic and its user that much stronger."

"Brilliant."

Bailey's eyes widened as she watched Mrs. Brody with reverence. Between those two, I bet there wasn't any spell they couldn't do.

After finishing up setting out the ingredients, Bailey helped her crush the necessary herbs and other such things in the bowls. We all sat back and watched the two at work, knowing full well we'd just get in the way if we tried to help.

Momma cat jumped from Bailey's lap onto the table and joined her kitten in front of Rory, who took turns scratching behind each cat's ears.

"We'll need a map," Mrs. Brody said, her eyes still fixated on her task in front of her.

"Uh, I can print one out?" I suggested. "How big does it need to be?"

"Large enough to not write off anywhere," Bailey said.

"So, the United States maybe?"

"But then detailed enough to see addresses," she continued.

"So, downtown Brimstone Bay?" I sighed. This wasn't going to be easy. I rubbed my temples again to try and eradicate the pressure headache I could feel growing between my ears.

"I've got an idea," Jane offered. She then jumped from her seat and ran up the stairs.

"Better be a massive map," I muttered to myself. Soot purred and flopped on the table in front of me, rolling onto his back, asking for tummy rubs.

"You're a spoiled little thing, you know that?" I whispered to him as I scratched his belly. His purring grew louder.

Jane came bounding back down the stairs a moment later with her iPad tucked under one arm.

"Here we go," she said, placing the tablet on the table. "We can zoom in and out as we need."

I laughed. "You serious? That's hilarious."

Bailey looked up to Mrs. Brody. "Will it work?"

She shrugged in reply. "Well, it's not exactly been done before, but we are modern witches, so…"

She pulled the tablet closer and Jane went to sit beside her to help her figure out the controls.

Bailey continued to grind herbs in her bowl, then once the map had been brought up on the screen, she pushed her bowl in front of Mrs. Brody, who placed all the mixtures in the middle of a spread-out cloth. She then folded the cloth up, placed it in a black ceramic bowl with perforations in its side, and covered it with the lid. With a wave of her hand over the bowl, scented smoke began emanating from it.

She carefully placed the bowl on the far side of the tablet, and Bailey switched off the lights above us with a wave of her own hand.

"Okay, focus on the magic you all recognized," Mrs. Brody said. "Either the effect it had on Trey's body, or perhaps the smoke that emanated from the cookie when I tested it for magic. Or even the aura you see now. Whatever part sticks strongest in each of your memories, focus on that."

I pictured the blue lines spreading across Trey's lifeless face. I felt a pang of sadness, especially for Jordan, but I pushed it aside. We had more pressing things to worry about than someone's feelings at the moment.

Mrs. Brody removed her necklace and held it out over the tablet. I never noticed it before, as it was usually tucked under her high-collared shirts, but the necklace had a tarnished silver symbol hanging from it. I couldn't quite make out what it was in the dark, but my guess was that it was something witchy.

I closed my eyes and focused on the magic as she began her incantations. The energy in the room immediately changed, and the air felt heavy. The smoke from the bowl was intoxicating, and I could feel myself being surrounded by powerful magic.

"The map, dear," Mrs. Brody said after a long moment of silence.

I opened my eyes to see Jane scrambling with the iPad screen. The necklace was pulled at an angle in the air toward the bottom corner of the screen, and Jane zoomed in towards where the necklace was pointing. Every time the screen adjusted or zoomed in, the necklace circled around a few more times and then settled once more.

I imagined one of those great old Halloween

movies like Hocus Pocus being remade today. I doubted anyone would believe them casting spells on iPads. It just simply looked ridiculous. I contained my laughter, but it was tough.

After a few more adjustments to the map app on the iPad, the necklace focused in on New York City.

I looked up and met eye contact with Bailey, who returned my worried look. Trey's largest restaurant was in New York, so it wasn't too far of a stretch to assume that's where the spell came from. I just hoped it had nothing to do with me. I had a way of attracting crazy.

"Zoom in closer," I said as the necklace began to circle again.

After a few more adjustments, the necklace settled on a small narrow building on Mulberry Street in Chinatown.

I marked the address in my phone, then looked up at four sets of eyes looking back at me.

I stared at them in turn, trying to think of what to say.

I shrugged. "Looks like we're going to New York."

CHAPTER SEVEN

My alarm woke me early the next morning.

My brain was groggy and my body was still sore. It wasn't until I stretched and finally opened my eyes that the events of the previous night came crashing down on me hard.

Trey was dead, and the person who cast the spell that killed him was in New York. Great.

I reluctantly pushed myself out of bed to prepare for the day. I had a feeling this week at work was going to be insane, given the event and the death, and I really needed to prove myself against Zack. I didn't see him at the party last night, so, hopefully, I'll be the one with the scoop.

As I got dressed, I remembered that Sheriff Reese wanted a full update first thing in the morning. I mentally scrambled my memories together and hoped that I didn't sound too crazy for when I'd tell him about the dark magic.

It would be good to see Mrs. Pots, too. The poor woman would have been stuck at the local jail all night with the officers, and that couldn't have been comfortable. The faster we figured this out, the better.

I pulled on my favorite pair of torn skinny jeans and a t-shirt, and went to see if the girls were awake.

Surprisingly, the house was lively—very unnatural for seven in the morning—and I could smell breakfast wafting up from downstairs.

I laughed to myself. The girls never left the house until they ate a complete breakfast. It was their number one rule.

Me, I would happily run on coffee and a piece of leftover pizza, given the chance.

The girls were all the way down in Mrs. Brody's basement apartment, but when I got there, I saw no sign of Mrs. Brody.

"Brody still sleeping?" I asked, trying to conceal a loud yawn with the back of my free hand. The other was already reaching for the coffee pot on the counter.

Bailey shook her head. "She's with Mrs. Pots at the Sheriff's office."

"Already?" I checked the time on my phone. Yep, it was still just past seven o'clock.

"I didn't think they allowed visitors until after nine?"

Rory shrugged. "You try stopping Mrs. Brody when she wants something."

I filled a coffee mug to the brim and joined the girls around the table. "Fair point."

The items from the tracking spell last night were still scattered around the table, and I could still smell the scent of the herbs that were burned. I had a feeling that smell would take a while to dissipate.

The coffee was hot and glorious, and instantly invigorated me. It didn't take long for me to drain the mug.

"Another coffee?" Rory asked, shaking her head as she brought over the coffee pot. "You know, you really should cut back on your caffeine intake."

"You really should cut back on your…" I tried to think of a comeback, but came up dry.

"Good one."

I laughed. "Too early for comebacks. I'll get back to you on that one later."

"Mmm hmm," Rory said. She sat down next to me after refilling my mug.

"Shall we go visit Mrs. Pots?" I asked, sipping this coffee more slowly than the one I had just inhaled.

"Yeah, I guess so," Bailey said. "It makes me so angry that they're holding her there."

"Same," Jane said. "We all know she's innocent.

Sheriff Reese knows, as well. This whole thing is stupid."

I shrugged. "He can't let her off just because it's stupid. We need to solve this, and fast."

The girls agreed.

IT DIDN'T TAKE us long to get to the Sheriff's office. It wasn't even eight o'clock yet, but after knocking frantically for a few minutes on the front door, Sheriff Reese resigned to letting us in.

"Thanks, Sheriff," Rory cooed as we pranced into the precinct.

"That for me?" Sheriff Reese eyed the large thermos of coffee I was carrying.

"Nope." I walked by him towards the front counter, which was empty at that time of morning, and set it down. "It's for Mrs. Pots. Where is she?"

"My office."

I led the girls down the hall towards the Sheriff's office. I was surprised to see Mrs. Brody and Mrs. Pots sitting on the couch by the far wall, talking enthusiastically amongst themselves.

"I brought coffee," I said as I entered the room.

"Oh, how lovely," Mrs. Pots announced, clapping her hands in glee.

"You look rather chipper given the fact that you just spent the night in the precinct."

Mrs. Pots waved me away with one hand as she poured the coffee from the thermos into a small Styrofoam cup she grabbed from the side cupboard. "Oh, it's nothing, dear. Have to make the best of our situations, don't we? Besides, it's such a lovely space."

She practically bounced back to the couch with a smile on her face.

I eyed Mrs. Brody, who was looking down at her feet rather suspiciously.

When I knew the Sheriff was out of ear shot, I scolded her, "What did you do?"

She shrugged. "Oh, nothing, dear. Just a teensy, weensy spell to liven the mood."

Mrs. Pots was humming to herself, fully content in her current situation.

I rolled my eyes. "This is serious, Mrs. Brody."

"Oh, hush now, girl. The poor woman needed some cheering up. It's not exactly the Hilton in here."

"Did she spend the night behind bars?"

Mrs. Brody nodded. "She was in the back room, locked away when I arrived this morning. Poor dear. At least, she had a warm bed to sleep in. Rather lonely place to spend the night, though."

I sighed and joined them on a chair next to the sofa. The girls pulled in chairs from the hallway and completed the circle.

"What did you give her?" Rory asked, trying not

to laugh when Mrs. Pots began singing opera softly to herself.

"Oh, never you mind," Mrs. Brody snapped.

I shrugged. "Just don't let this interfere with the investigation."

"Don't be ridiculous," Mrs. Brody said to me, grabbing the coffee I had just poured from my hands.

"Hey, that was mine," I said.

"Shouldn't you girls be off to New York?"

I shook my head. "I have to go in to work today. We'll leave tomorrow."

"Can't you just call in sick?" Jane asked.

I laughed. "You guys really don't know what it's like to work for a living, do you?"

They all shrugged. I still hadn't figured out how these girls can get away with not having jobs. Whenever I brought it up, they always changed the subject. I'll get to the bottom of it one of these days. They couldn't all come from a long line of rich witches, could they?

I eyed them suspiciously, then turned my attention back to pouring myself another cup of coffee.

About fifteen minutes later, Sheriff Reese came in, accompanied by the Mayor.

"Hey, Mayor Scott," I smiled at him as he joined us in the room. We all shifted our chairs over to make room for two more.

The Mayor nodded to us, then turned his attention to Sheriff Reese.

"You better have something for me," he said. "We need to make this go away before things get out of hand."

"With all due respect, sir," the Sheriff said to the tall, ruggedly handsome man next to him. "I'm in charge of this investigation, and I'm the one who will be managing the situation."

The Sheriff's cheeks became a light pink. The Sheriff was, in fact, older than the Mayor, but Mayor Scott had such a powerful presence, it was hard not to feel small around him.

The Mayor nodded. "You're right, my apologies. This whole thing just has me worried. I can't imagine what the press will say."

He eyed me after saying that last bit. I shrugged back at him and sipped my coffee. Truthfully, I had no idea what the paper would write. I didn't seem to have much control over anything anymore. I just hoped I could beat Zack to the chase.

"So, can anyone please explain further what happened last night?" Sheriff Reese asked. "I got the lab results back from the cookie an hour ago, and they came up clean." He was half bent over his desk, rubbing his forehead with his thumbs. It didn't look like he got any sleep last night.

I sighed, then glanced up to Mayor Scott. He nodded to me, encouraging me to speak.

"Well," I started. "We found magic. Dark magic." The Sheriff rolled his eyes, but let me continue.

"We traced it back to New York."

Mayor Scott shifted in his seat. "New York? How?"

"And don't you dare say Facebook," the Sheriff added.

I eyed the Mayor, then continued. "We found a way to track where the magic came from. We narrowed it down to a small building in New York City."

"Okay, I'll bite," Sheriff Reese said. "How did you trace it?"

"Tracking spell," I said simply.

"Right." He continued to rub his temples. "Well, seeing as that's all we've got to work with, we might as well check it out."

"I think it's best if you sit this one out, Sheriff," Mayor Scott said. The Sheriff glared at him, then finally nodded. "Best to leave the magic stuff to the professionals."

"So, you think the poisoned cookie came from New York?" Sheriff Reese asked.

"No, I gave him the cookie," Mrs. Pots chimed in. She then giggled and continued humming to herself.

The Sheriff narrowed his eyes. "Did you poison the cookie?"

"Of course, not, stupid man," she sang back.

"Okay, what the hell is with Mrs. Pots?" Mayor Scott asked, looking around at us one by one.

I shrugged. "Guess the stress of spending the night locked away have really gotten to her. The poor, poor woman."

The Mayor glared at me, but I could tell by his expression that he knew arguing about it was a lost cause, so he let it drop.

"Do you girls have anything concrete to support your claim that Mrs. Pots didn't have anything to do with the murder?" Sheriff Reese asked.

We all shook our heads.

"No, not yet," I said. "But we will. Soon."

"Then, unfortunately, we'll have to keep her here until we have more to go on. Not only do we have an eye witness, but she's admitting full well she's the one who gave Trey the cookie that killed him."

Now it was my turn to rub my temples. "The witness is the widow, so her emotions are certainly clouding her judgment. And Mrs. Pots was running the dessert table, so, of course, she gave him the cookie. But that means absolutely nothing, given the fact that you know she wasn't the one to poison it."

"We don't know that for sure," he snapped back at me. "We're keeping her here until you find something. So, you better hurry up."

Mrs. Pots bounced on the couch. "Oh, goodie, another sleep over."

I eyed Mrs. Pots, then glanced back to Sheriff Reese. "Don't worry, we'll figure this out."

We had to, as the alternative would be Mrs. Pots being sent to state prison for murder. Our simply denying her involvement based on character wasn't going to be strong enough once the higher-ups got involved. We had to act, and fast.

CHAPTER EIGHT

THE WALK FROM THE SHERIFF'S OFFICE TO MY office was long. The girls decided to stay with Mrs. Pots for the day, and as Rory was the one with the car, I winded up having to walk all the way back to work.

Luckily, the sun was out, and while the air was cool and crisp, it felt good to get some fresh air.

The walk also allowed me some time to think. If what Sheriff Reese said was true, then not only did we have one murder to solve, but other people may be at risk, too. If the cookie hadn't been meant for Trey, then who knows who the target recipient was. I chewed by lip as I walked, trying not to think too hard about whether it was meant for one of us. The only thing that calmed that thought was the hope that we would have been able to sense the magic in the cookie before it poisoned us.

On that thought, it made sense that the target would not have been a witch. At least, that cuts out those of us in the house.

I put my headphones on to listen to music, and increased my pace to a jog. It'd been ages since I'd gone running around the bay, and I missed the feeling of the air on my face. It was calming, and I did my best thinking when I ran. With any luck, a brisk jog back to work might stimulate some brilliant ideas for the article I was about to write about the event.

As it turned out, my mind came up blank. I got so lost in my own thoughts that before I knew it, I had arrived in town and was almost at the office. I slowed down and stretched my arms above my head as I walked, relishing in the feeling of using my muscles for once. Being a journalist means lots of butt-in-chair time, and while my fingers were getting strong from typing so much, the rest of my body really felt the hit.

I pulled my ear buds out, but still heard music as I approached my office door and noticed it was coming from the cafe downstairs. The windows were still covered in newsprint, but I walked up to the door anyway and placed my ear against the glass. I could faintly hear Metallica playing, and knew that Jordan must be inside. I knocked softly, partially not wanting to disturb him in the off chance that he's sleeping in there, and partially because a part of me didn't want to face him right now. His good friend had just died, and I had no idea what to say to him. I felt that nothing I did would help, and I didn't want to make things worse by asking him about it.

After a few moments, I withdrew and rummaged through my bag to find my keys to the office door, which was right next to the door to the cafe. It was exceptionally convenient having an unlimited source of caffeine this close to the office. I was sad at the thought that Mr. Bramley's cafe would never be there in the same way again.

The door to the cafe opened as I was still looking for my keys and Jordan's tired face poked out from the doorway to look at me. "Oh. Hey, River."

I smiled and turned to look at him. "Hey," was all I managed to say. I opened my mouth to say more, but I was caught up dry. I closed my lips and looked at him with the most sympathetic expression I could manage.

"Want to come in?" he asked, pushing the door open wider.

"Oh, sure," I said. I dropped the keys back into my bag and followed Jordan inside.

"Holy crap," I said, taking in the scene around me. "Were you up all night?" The entire renovation looked nearly complete. The walls had been painted, the new counter had been installed and polished, and the floors had been scrubbed.

He rubbed his eyes, then nodded. "Yeah, I

couldn't sleep after last night." He sat down in one of the booths and scooted over so I could come sit beside him.

"I get that," I said. "You did a good job."

Jordan smiled. It was a half-smile, and he had a haunted look about him, but it was a smile nonetheless. I squeezed his hand and smiled back.

"We're going to find out who did this," I said.

He nodded. "I'm more worried about the why part." Jordan looked down at his feet then closed his eyes. I could tell that he was truly heartbroken about his friend.

"I'm so sorry, Jordan."

We sat in silence together, his hands resting in mine. After a few moments, he squeezed my hands back, then stretched and shook his head.

"There's no sense feeling sorry for myself about it," he finally said. "It's done, and we can't change that fact. What I can do, though, is finish setting up this restaurant and making it the best it can be."

I gaped at him. "You're going through with the restaurant?"

He nodded. "It was Trey's dream, and I'm going to see it through. Besides, Grace was half the talent and she can help me run the place."

I laughed at that, knowing full well that Grace wouldn't agree to living in this small town in a million years. "Good luck with making her stay. Where is she, anyways?"

Jordan sighed. "She went back to the city to be with her family. It was too hard for her to stay here."

"I don't blame her," I said. "I'd have done the same. The poor girl."

Jordan shook his head and yawned. "She left last night. Couldn't handle being here without him. I can't imagine what she's feeling right now."

"I'll call her sister and check up on her today, see how Grace is doing."

"That would be great, thank you."

I stood up and pulled Jordan up with me. "You're going to get through this, you know."

He nodded. "Yeah, I know. It's just a lot to handle."

"I know. But you've got the restaurant to keep you busy. I'll come down and help out when I can, okay?"

He smiled at me and pulled me in close and kissed me.

I couldn't help the wide grin that spread over my face, and my knees buckled a little bit. I recovered quickly, grabbing hold of his arm to stabilize myself.

"What was that?" Jordan asked.

"Nothing."

"Did I just make you weak at the knees?"

"No," I said hurriedly. "Nope, just tripped."

"Liar. I made you swoon." He was grinning down at me, and I could feel my cheeks growing warm.

"Shut up. No, you didn't." Oh, my God, I was humiliated. I was a grown woman, not some stupid high school girl who faints when a cute boy walks by. At least, this seemed to cheer him up.

"Well, why don't I take you out for dinner tonight. I'll see if I can make it happen again."

I shook my head. "Nope, nothing to happen again. I didn't swoon. Your traumatized mind is imagining things. It's common after an event like last night…" I trailed off, trying not to sound like a mumbling lunatic.

"Mmm hmm, sure."

"Well, I gotta go," I said quickly, then turned to leave.

Jordan grabbed my arm and pulled me back and kissed me again. This time I locked my knees to be sure I wouldn't collapse like an idiot again.

"So, dinner tonight?"

I nodded. "Yeah, it's a date."

THE DOOR to the Brimstone Press office was unlocked when I left the cafe. Or, restaurant, I knew I should start calling it. That's going to be a hard thing to adjust to.

The lights were on, and JoAnn was busy typing away at her computer when I entered our tiny second floor office.

"Hey, you're up early," I commented as I threw my bag down on the chair next to her desk.

She smiled up at me. "So are you. Coffee?"

My jaw dropped at the sight of two large steaming hot takeout coffees on her desk.

"For me?" I asked, then beamed wildly when she nodded. "Where did you find such a glorious thing?"

JoAnn laughed. "What with the cafe downstairs closed, a girl's gotta be resourceful." I raised my eyebrow at her as a mischievous look crossed her face. I sipped my coffee and waited for her to continue.

"The inn. I got it at the inn," she said, rolling her eyes at my intent expression. Ah, I was hoping she was going to say a new coffee shop had opened up nearby or something. I'd just have to make a point of ensuring Jordan's place is equipped with excellent coffee. I made a mental note of expressing the importance of this to him next time we speak.

I pulled up another chair and set my laptop on the edge of JoAnn's desk.

"I'll finish that article on the party today for you," I said. "I'm assuming you want me to touch on the murder, as well." I made it a statement and not a question, hoping she would just agree and let me write the damn thing.

JoAnn shook her head. "Don't worry about that, Zack's going to cover the murder."

I sighed and rubbed my temples. "You know, just

because I don't have as much experience as he does, doesn't mean I'm completely useless."

She eyed me, but held her silence.

"Please," I continued. "Let me help. Let me be useful. I've felt like an idiot since he arrived, writing nothing but birthday updates and yesterday's news." There, I had said it. I wasn't sure what prompted me to spill my thoughts at that moment, but I was proud of myself for at least admitting my feelings to her.

JoAnn sat back in her seat and folded her fingers together on her desk. "I'm sorry you feel that way," she began, "but you must know that this is nothing against you or your skills. You are a very talented journalist, but we brought Zack on because of his extensive experience in things like this. We want to be put on the map as a professional news organization, and we needed that little extra push to get us there."

After I didn't reply, she continued, "You'll get your chance again, River. Don't worry. Just hold tight for now."

I sighed. "Fine. Yes, of course. I'm sorry, I'm just really tired. It's been a long night."

She nodded. "Oh, I hear ya." She then went back to typing at her computer.

"Did you end up making it to the party?" I asked, trying to rack my brain to remember if I even saw her there last night.

"Yes, just barely, though," she said. "Zack and I

arrived late, just before the murder happened, unfortunately. We left straight away, not wanting to get in anyone's way."

I nodded. "Thanks for that," I said. "Took a while for Mrs. Brody to clear out the yard."

"I expect you'll be filling Zack in on the details," she said after a pause. "He should be in later today. In the meantime, do you mind finishing up his article on the restaurant opening downstairs? I'm going to be moving him from that coverage to the murder, and it would be great if you could help wrap that one up."

"Sure, no problem," I said. At least, this would give me something to focus on.

After a few more minutes of frantic typing, JoAnn shut off her computer and put on her coat. "I need to go out of town for the day. Let me know if you need anything. Try and get that article done by this evening, if possible. You can e-mail me what you've got when you're done."

"Sounds good. See ya." She waved her hand back at me as she left the office. I got up and locked the door behind her. I didn't want anyone else bothering me as I wrote. I knew that anyone who would possible come bother me had their own set of keys, but for some reason knowing the door was locked offered a small bit of comfort.

I sighed, then pushed JoAnn's stuff to the side of her desk and took over the work space.

I would have to wait until Zack got to the office to really get started on his article, so I figured I might as well finish my bit about the party. I'd have to leave out the details about the end of the night, but I could at least talk about the preparations that went into it, and maybe a bit on the history of the party.

I sighed out loud to myself, and resigned to typing up the lame article.

About an hour went by, and Zack still hadn't arrived. I was lost in my thoughts, typing away at the computer, when a loud buzzing made my jump.

My heart raced and I looked around the room for the source of the noise, and traced it over to Zack's desk. My desk, really, but whatever.

I went over to find the source of the buzzing, more so just because I wanted it to stop than the fact that I was curious as to what it was, and found Zack's phone ringing in the top drawer of his desk.

I blinked a few times as I stared at the phone in my hand, seeing the name "Grace" flash on the screen. I stared at the device, trying to figure out why Grace would be calling Zack's number. Could this be Trey's phone, maybe? It's not out of the question for the newspaper to collect things for research on an article. Maybe Grace was trying to track down where his phone had gone to?

The sound of footsteps came from beyond the door, and I frantically scrambled to put the phone back where

I found it and close the drawer. Zack walked into the office just as I barely had a chance to step away from his desk, and my heart was racing a mile a minute.

"Oh, hey Zack," I tried to sound cool.

He nodded to me, then walked over to his desk. "Sup?"

I shrugged and went back to my chair and pretended to be in the middle of something on my computer. "Nothing. You know, just the usual."

"Cool. I'm just stopping by, have an appointment in a bit."

"'Kay," I said, eyeing him as he rummaged through the piles of papers on his desk, moving random items aside. "Do you mind sending me your stuff on the restaurant? JoAnn wants me to finish it up for you."

"Oh, yeah," he said, then swore under his breath as he kept moving things around his desk. "Sure. No problem. Will send them in a bit."

"Thanks."

Zack opened the top drawer, then blew out a sigh. "Jesus, there it is. Thought I'd lost it." He pulled out the phone from the drawer and slid it into his back pocket.

I saluted him in a mocking gesture. "Always do," I muttered.

"Oh, River," he turned back towards me as he stepped out the door. "You looked good last night.

You look good with makeup on, you should wear it more often."

I didn't even see him last night, so I had no idea when he had the chance to check out my makeup. I ignored him and rolled my eyes. "You'd look better with a bag over your head," I muttered to myself.

"What was that?" he asked.

"Nothing. Stay cool."

He winked at me, then I watched him leave as his phone flashed in his back pocket.

CHAPTER NINE

"YOU READY TO GO?" BAILEY ASKED AS SHE CAME bounding into my room with Momma cat in her arms.

"Go where?" I asked.

She stared at me for a long moment, then rolled her eyes. "Honestly, River. Where has your brain been all day?"

I shrugged, still not realizing what she was talking about.

After I didn't answer, she continued, "New York, of course."

"Ah." In truth, I had completely forgotten we had agreed to go to New York. I was too preoccupied thinking about what I saw on Zack's phone, that I totally forgot we were going on a road trip.

"Rory's got the car all ready. Have you packed?"

I looked at the time on my phone. It was just past noon. "You realize it's at least a six hour drive, right?"

Bailey nodded and smiled. "Yep, so we better get going, then."

I sighed. "Alright, I'll get my things ready. Be down in fifteen?"

Bailey beamed, then set the giant white cat down on my bed. "Hurry! We're all excited to go."

"You betcha," I said with a forced smile. I threw myself back on my bed when she left and stared up at the ceiling. My brain was having trouble processing the events of the past twenty-four hours. Everything seemed like a whirlwind, and I was starting to lose my mind a little bit.

I packed up my laptop and a change of clothes, tossed my toothbrush and a towel into my bag, and then went to add extra food into the cat bowls down the hall. That should hold them over for a day or two, hopefully. Although, with the amount of food that Momma cat was eating lately, I added in a few extra scoops for good measure. That cat sure liked to eat.

I looked around for Soot to give him a goodbye scratch, but he was off somewhere, likely causing trouble with one of the neighbors or stealing food from Mrs. Brody downstairs.

"See you guys later," I said out loud to no one in particular. Who knew, maybe the cats had supernatural hearing and could understand English. You never know.

I finally joined the girls downstairs, who were already packed away in the car and ready to go, and I grudgingly threw my bag in the trunk and took my place in the passenger seat.

"Road trip!" Bailey called from the back seat as Rory reversed the car down the driveway.

I laughed and couldn't help but absorb some of their enthusiasm. We had never gone away together, and it would be fun to hang out with the girls outside of the house. There weren't exactly many clubs, or much of a nightlife in Brimstone Bay, and we often stayed in on the weekends and just hung out together at home with a couple of beers. I was looking forward to being back in the middle of everything in New York.

We were lucky in that it was mid-day on a Monday and there wasn't much traffic. It was smooth sailing all the way from Brimstone Bay down the coast. We spent the hours chatting away about life and boys and all that typical stuff. I had to admit, I was having a pretty good time.

"Oh, crap," I said as I remembered something. I threw my head back against the headrest and sighed a loud and exasperated sigh to myself. "I totally forgot."

"What? Don't tell me you forgot something at home," Rory said from the driver's seat.

"No," I sighed again. "I told Jordan I'd go for dinner with him tonight. I totally forgot."

"Ouuu, so, are you guys officially dating now?" Bailey asked.

I shook my head. "No. Not really. I dunno." I took my phone out of my bag and stared at it for a long minute, trying to figure out what I would say to Jordan.

"River and Officer O'Riley," Bailey sang. "River and O'Riley. It's catchy!"

"OH!" Rory screeched. "We can call you guys RiRi. It's perfect"

The girls all laughed and I suppressed a groan.

"Isn't that a Kardashian or something?" I asked.

Rory rolled her eyes. "Honestly, River. It's Rihanna."

I laughed. "What's the difference?"

"What's the difference?" Rory gasped. "You can't be serious."

Bailey and Jane were in hysterics in the back seat.

I shrugged and brought up the messages app on my phone.

"We'll forgive you this once," Bailey said. "But only if you invite your sexy cop over to the house for dinner."

"Does he have any hot cop friends?" Rory asked.

"First of all, he's not a cop anymore," I said.

"Second, I'm not bringing him anywhere near you psychos."

"Should have asked him to come on the girl's trip," Jane teased. "We could have braided that beautiful long blonde hair of his."

I rolled my eyes, then began texting a lengthy apology to Jordan about our date.

After a few minutes, my phone buzzed back as he replied to my message. I sighed in relief as I read his text. He understood, of course, and said he had stuff to do tonight, anyway.

"You tell him why we're going?" Bailey asked.

I shook my head again. "No, best keep that to ourselves for now."

"Good idea," Rory agreed. "Keep it between the bitches."

I nudged her with my elbow. "Hey."

She chuckled. "I mean witches." I laughed, then turned up the volume on the stereo. I didn't recognize half the music that was playing, but Rory insisted they were all modern hits. A song same on drawling on about something to do with bling and some sort of a hotline, and I turned the stereo back down.

"What is that crap?" I asked, completely not believing her that this stuff was popular.

Rory rolled her eyes. "That's Drake. Learn to love it."

"Fat chance."

"Isn't he dating RiRi?" Bailey said.

"Who?"

"Okay, seriously, River," Rory said. "We just talked about this. Get with the times!"

"Nah, I'm good," I laughed.

We chatted and listened to music the rest of the ride down, and after stopping—once for a snack and gas break—we reached the city a little past seven.

"Where are we staying?" I asked as the skyscrapers of New York City appeared in the distance.

After a few long moments of silence, Rory shrugged. "We were hoping you would know somewhere."

"Seriously? You guys didn't plan for a place to stay?" I laughed.

"We can just drop into a bed and breakfast or something, can't we?" Bailey asked.

I turned to look at the girls in the back seat. "This isn't Brimstone Bay. Have you guys even been to New York before?"

Both girls looked at each other, then shook their heads.

I sighed. "I'll make some calls."

I spent the last leg of the trip calling everyone I still knew in the city. Finally, I got through to Emily, Grace's younger sister, and she agreed to let us come stay with her in her apartment downtown. Luckily, it was pretty close to the shop we were going to, so things couldn't have worked out much better. I'm was glad I was going to get the chance to see Emily, as it would give us a chance to talk about Grace. I really hoped she was doing okay.

"Emily has got a small apartment just outside of Chinatown," I said. I reached for Rory's phone and input the address into her GPS.

New York City was an expensive city to live in, and the apartments weren't known to be spacious. It would be a tight fit, but I was looking forward to a night of just hanging out. It felt good to be going back to the city.

It took us a while to find parking after arriving in Manhattan. We ended up finding a sketchy parking lot on a corner about six blocks away, and had to lug our bags through the busy streets all the way back to Emily's apartment.

Luckily, after not even a minute of breathing in the New York air, my city aggression flooded back in and I led the way, plowing through the busy streets like no body's business. It felt like a renewed sense of confidence. I was definitely ready to tackle whatever surprises this trip has to throw at us.

Emily was waiting for us at the front door of her apartment building and eagerly led us up the five flights of stairs to her tiny apartment.

After settling in, she handed each of us a beer and we climbed up to the rooftop patio. The building was only ten stories, so the view didn't go very far, but the city sounds reverberating off the surrounding buildings electrified the atmosphere. I smiled to myself at the familiar sounds: honking cab horns, a thousand muffled conversations, echoing music from the surrounding clubs and restaurants. It was great to be back, but it didn't take long to feel glad that I had found a more peaceful place to live. I loved the bustle of the city, but it sure was nice to be somewhere quiet for once.

"So, what brings you guys to New York?" Emily asked as we each made our own make-shift seats with stuff that was scattered around the roof. It wasn't an official patio up here, but you could tell it was heavily used. A few potted plants were scattered around the perimeter of the roof, and there were a few broken chairs and crates lying around.

"We came to find, er…" Rory began. "We came to find someone."

"It's okay," I told her. "Emily knows all about the witch stuff. You'll find it's a lot more open here in the city."

Emily beamed. "I actually just got a job at Shine. One of the underground paranormal bars just down the street. I'm surrounded by magic users every day, pretty much, so, you don't have to worry about keeping any secrets from me."

"That's amazing!" I said. "I love that place. Grace must be super jealous." Grace had spent nearly every weekend in that club when I lived in

New York. In the past few years, I think she had managed to date at least half of the regulars who came through, and pretty much all of the staff. That girl liked her shifter men.

"Yeah, she came to see me last night."

I raised my eyebrow. "Oh, yeah? So, she's back in New York, then. How is she doing?"

Emily sighed. "She just stopped by on her way out of town. She's having a really hard time. She booked herself into a widow's grief retreat for counselling. She'll never admit that to you, though. She's putting on a brave face. You know how she is. I hope the counselling helps her get through this."

"It's so tragic," Bailey said. "I can't imagine losing someone you love at such a young age. They had their whole lives ahead of them."

"It has completely shocked all of us. The whole family is heartbroken. We all loved Trey like a brother. He was such a great guy."

Emily wiped away the tears that had welled up in her eyes. "And I have no idea what Grace plans to do with the restaurants now. She has no hope in running them all on her own. Trey was the one who managed all of that stuff. She's lost without him."

"She's a smart girl, she'll figure it out," I smiled. As far as I understood, Trey had been wanting to scale down the business for a while. With any luck, he may have already started the process and Grace would only have to worry about her own restaurant here in New York.

"So, what did you guys say you were doing here?"

"We're hoping to get more information about who or what killed Trey," I said.

Emily nodded and regained her composure. "Do you have any leads?"

"Some," I nodded. "We're going to check out a shop tomorrow. Then, hopefully, we'll have what we need and can head back home afterward."

"Well, then, might as well enjoy tonight as much as we can before you get down to business tomorrow!" Emily was basically bouncing on her heals, she looked so excited. I was glad to be able to offer her a distraction through this hard time for her family, at least.

"What do you have in mind?" Bailey asked. She was barely able to contain the excitement growing on her face as well. Bailey often talked about going to New York, but, as far as I knew, she had never even left Maine.

"Do you guys want to go to Shine?"

I glanced at my housemates, then back to Emily. "We didn't bring anything fancy to wear."

Emily shrugged. "It's okay, it's a Monday night. It's more of a bar on weeknights. You'll be fine in what you're wearing."

Bailey, Jane, and Rory looked like they were

about to explode, they were so excited. We didn't even have a night club in town, let alone one that catered to paranormals.

"Alright, looks like we're going to Shine," I laughed.

After finishing our beers, Emily lent us some jewelry and we all headed out for a night on the town.

The club was only a few blocks away, and it was about nine o'clock by the time we got there. The club itself was underground and we had to take a set of stairs in the back alley behind a butcher shop to get there. They did a good job of keeping the club off the radar of normal people walking by. It seemed really sketchy from the outside, and I could tell the girls were nervous about going in, but the club itself inside was actually really nice and the girls were pleasantly surprised.

The music wasn't too loud, and the atmosphere was actually quite relaxed. It wasn't a typical night club you go out to the dance like crazy on the weekends. It really did have a bar-like vibe to it, and most people were sitting around the bar chatting. I'd only been here on weekends before, and much preferred it like this.

We found a table near the bar and ordered a round of drinks, and Emily started chatting with the girls and they all started to get to know each other.

There was something nagging the back of my

mind, and I excused myself from the table to go make a phone call in the back room. On normal weekends, the back rooms were reserved for parties, but, as it was Monday night, they were empty. I brought out my phone and dialed Jordan's number. I was relieved when he answered after the first ring.

I couldn't stop thinking about seeing Grace's name flashing on Zack's phone back in the office. I'm sure it was nothing, but I really wanted to get to the bottom of it.

"I just wanted to say sorry again for bailing on dinner tonight," I told him.

"It's okay, River, I understand. You busy with your housemates?"

"Actually, we're in New York. Surprise girl's trip."

"That's fun. You having a good time?"

"Yeah, I am. It's nice being back in the city." I paused for a moment. "Hey, look, there's something I wanted to ask you."

"What's that?"

"Can you think of any reason why Grace would be calling Zack?"

He didn't say anything for a minute, obviously expecting my question to be something else. "The guy you work with?" he finally asked.

"Yeah."

"Uh… Well, he called the shop a few times. Had

some questions about the restaurant and other things. Grace was probably just returning a call. Why?"

"No reason," I said, blowing out a sigh. "Something was just nagging me."

"River, I know you work at the paper and all, but you really shouldn't stress yourself out by getting involved in all of this. Just let the cops do their thing." I knew he was trying to help, but he really didn't seem to understand why I needed to get involved. After I didn't answer, he went on. "Have you seen Grace?"

I shook my head, then remembered he couldn't see me. "No, but we're staying with her sister. Sounds like Grace just wants to be alone right now. I don't blame her." I left out the bit about the counselling retreat, as I figured it wasn't our business.

"Me neither. I can't imagine what she's going through right now."

"Yeah. What are you going to do with your place now that Trey's gone?"

"My plans haven't changed. I get the impression Grace doesn't want anything to do with the restaurant, being stuck in a small town, and all that. When she's settled down a bit, I'll have to talk to her about our plan going forward. As his wife, she technically owns his restaurants now."

"Yeah, I guess she does. Poor girl's going to have a lot to deal with."

"She will, indeed. Hey, River, just focus on having fun in the city, okay? Please don't worry about any of this. I know Trey wouldn't want any of us to ruin our lives over this."

"Yeah, maybe," I said. I didn't want him to worry about me. "We'll probably head home tomorrow. Can we reschedule dinner for then?"

"Wouldn't miss it for the world."

I felt butterflies in my stomach as I hung up the phone. Not that I wanted to admit it to myself, but that man really had an effect on me. A strong one. And I felt like a giddy schoolgirl whenever I talked to him. Good thing he wasn't around to see me blush this time. It was strange. We've kissed, and that seemed completely normal and comfortable, yet I can't bring up the courage to actually ask him out officially.

I lingered in the back room for a few minutes, trying to subside the nagging in my mind about Grace's phone call. Could Zack be trying to talk to her for reasons that go beyond his article?

I felt a knot tighten in my stomach at the thought that he might be trying to dig for information as a way to cover something up. Zack was an ass, but I wasn't sure he was capable of murder. I thought back to seeing Grace's name on his phone. People do seem capable of doing terrible things for love. I pondered that thought for a moment, but was brought out of my trance by Emily calling from the other room.

"River!" Emily yelled. "Get your cute little but back here!"

I came back to the table to a pint of Guinness waiting for me.

"With a shot of vanilla vodka," Emily said as I reached for the glass. "Remember how we had them that night in our junior year?"

"Don't remember much of that night," I laughed. I took a sip and it tasted sweet and familiar, like toasted marshmallows and something smoky. "This is delicious."

"I'm getting one," Bailey said after I nearly inhaled half the pint in one go.

"Me, too," Rory said.

"So am I," Jane agreed.

I laughed at the girls as they went to the bar to order more drinks. They hadn't even finished what they had on the table.

We spent the rest of the evening chatting in the bar, and Rory and Jane even got some good dancing time in.

Bailey hung out at the bar most of the evening, flirting with the bartender. I hadn't seen that look in her eye since her infatuation with Ryan Bramley. It was nice seeing her move on to someone else, finally.

"That's Miles," Emily said as we watched Bailey

work her moves at the bar. "He's a cat shifter. Just started working here last month."

Miles was tall and handsome, with messy deep orange-brown hair and freckles. He had a tattoo on his upper arm that wrapped up part-way around his neck. I found it hard not to swoon as we watched him flirt back with Bailey.

"Nice catch, Bails," I said to Emily. She nodded and sipped her beer, neither of us wanting to look away from the outrageously handsome man.

Jane and Rory finally joined us back at the table once they had exhausted all of their dance moves.

It was a nice, low-key evening, and was just exactly what I needed. I even forgot the reason why we had come to New York for a while, and easily fell back into the rhythm of my old life for the evening.

It was nearly midnight when we headed back to Emily's apartment, which, for a Monday night, was pretty impressive for us. I'd gotten into the routine of waking up early, and being in bed by nine o'clock wasn't out of the ordinary for me lately.

Emily had set up cots for us to sleep in the living room, and the three of us nearly covered her entire floor. She had a pretty neat apartment, but it was barely bigger than my bedroom back at the house.

As we settled in for the night, we made plans to wake up early to visit the building we traced the spell to before the streets got too busy. We didn't chat for long, as we all crashed pretty hard.

Between the long drive, the multiple drinks, and the overly stressful week, I fell asleep as soon as my head hit the pillow.

CHAPTER TEN

THE SUN WOKE US EARLIER THAN MY ALARM, AS THE light reflecting off a neighboring building glared right into the living room where we slept.

I was glad for the earlier wake-up time as we had a big day ahead of us, and I had to mentally prepare for whatever interaction we might have when we arrived.

We had only managed to trace the spell to a certain building in Chinatown, but we didn't know how many units there would be, or even if it were shops or apartment.

With any luck, it would be a single shop, which would make our visit a lot easier. It would be a lot harder to make our way into a stranger's apartment. Not that we really planned on doing that.

Emily had ended the night with a double tequila shot, so we let her sleep in as we left quietly in the morning. Emily's apartment was only a few blocks from where we were headed, and it didn't take us long to walk. It was still early and most of the shops were closed, but the sun was up and city life was starting to pick up despite the early hour. We passed a few early risers on their way to work or to grab coffee or whatever their morning routine was.

As we approached the intersection near our destination, I noticed a flashing open sign on the front door of what appeared to be the only unit in the building we had come to see. Through the large windows, I could see that it was a laundromat, and a handful of people were inside doing laundry. I checked my phone and saw that it was still only six fifty-five. I realized I really took our in-house laundry for granted.

"Stop," I whispered urgently and pulled Bailey by the hood back against the side wall of the building we were passing. "Hide. All of you."

"What's going on?" Rory asked, following my lead and pressing her back up against the cold brick of the building.

I shushed her then turned sideways to peek around the corner of wall we were using as a shield, doing my best to stay as hidden as possible.

"Holy crap on a stick," I said. I squinted to make sure my eyes weren't deceiving me.

Zack freaking Brandon was walking out of the laundromat.

"It's Zack," I whispered. We were kitty corner across the intersection, so I was sure there was no way he could hear me, but I felt the need to whisper nonetheless.

"Who?" Jane asked. She bent down and poked her head around the wall beneath me. "Oh, what! The guy you work with?"

"No, way," Rory said, joining us at the edge of the wall. "Are you sure? There's no way."

He was wearing a jacket with the hood pulled up, but I was sure it was him. "Yeah, pretty sure."

"That could be anyone," Bailey said. She pushed my shoulders down so she could peer around the wall above my head. To anyone looking our way, we must have looked like a bunch of lunatics. Or stalkers, for that matter.

I pulled my phone from my jeans pocket and dialed Zack's number and held my breath. Sure enough, the guy standing outside the laundromat door reached for his phone and held it up in front of his face. His expression turned dark at the sight of my name of his phone.

"Shit," I swore under my breath. Zack glared at the phone for a long moment, then put it back in his pocket, ignoring my call.

"Jerk."

Zack then bolted down the street in the opposite direction to us, thankfully, and I watched as he hailed a cab and sped off in the distance.

Once he was safely out of sight, we stepped away from our hiding spot and stared at each other. We all shared the same blatantly confused expressions.

"So," I began. "That just happened."

Bailey scratched her head. "I don't understand."

I stared at the laundromat across the street and blinked, trying to make sense of what we had just witnessed.

"How does he know about this place?" Jane asked the obvious question we were all thinking.

I shook my head. "Better question is why the hell he came here."

Rory, Bailey, and Jane all nodded. "I've had a bad feeling about that guy since he first came to town," Bailey said. "Bad mojo, and all that sort of stuff."

I squeezed my eyes shut and rubbed my temples. "I'm going to need coffee if I have any hope of figuring this one out."

I led the way into the Starbucks we passed half a block back and ordered a triple Americano to go. I then sat down at one of the small tables outside and sipped my coffee in silence.

It took a solid five minutes of drinking coffee and processing what I had just witnessed before Bailey managed to pull me out of my daze and back to reality.

"Zack Brandon just visited the place we sourced

the dark magic that killed Trey," I recited out loud once Rory joined the rest of us at the table. She ordered some sort of whipped caramel atrocity that took seemingly forever to make. Those poor baristas. I swear, every year Starbucks comes up with even more obscure and complicated drinks that their young and underpaid staff had to magically whip up a million times a day for their cranky customers. I always made a point of tipping them well whenever I got coffee from there.

I shook my head in an attempt to bring my mind back to the task at hand. Zack. Zack Brandon and the laundromat. My issues with Starbucks could wait.

"We just saw Zack Brandon in the place the dark magic spell came from," I repeated.

Rory slowly shook her head back and forth in disbelief. "Can you think of any logical reason why he would be there?"

I took a long sip of my coffee and shrugged. "Nothing comes to mind."

"Maybe someone tipped him off and he came for the story?" Jane suggested.

I tried to remember the events that occurred following the murder last night. "No one else knows the location of the building apart from Mrs. Brody and us, and I highly doubt she would have spilled the beans to anyone."

"Could he have overheard us talking anywhere?" Rory asked.

I shrugged. "Doubt it." My head hurt, and I was having trouble processing everything. The awful truth that was hovering in my mind was a hard pill to swallow.

"Do you think Zack had something to do with the murder?" Bailey asked. "Did any of you even see him at the party?"

I shook my head. "No, I didn't see him."

"Neither did I," Jane said. "I don't think he came. I spent most of the night greeting people as they arrived, and I don't remember seeing him. Or your editor, for that matter."

I rubbed my eyes with the palms of my hands. "He's a misogynistic asshole, but I really don't think he's capable of murder," I answered. "I can't think of a motive. As far as I know, he hadn't even met the guy. He's still fairly new to town, and Trey and Grace only just moved to Brimstone Bay. The party would have been their first time meeting each other." I then remembered the thoughts I had about Zack at the bar last night.

"Unless…" I began.

"Unless?" Bailey asked.

"Isn't it suspicious that he didn't show up at the party?" I asked. "What if he was trying to find a way get close to Grace?"

Rory laughed. "Zack going after Grace? Isn't he dating your editor?"

I nodded. "Yeah, he is. Besides, I highly doubt

that she's his type. She's far too much of a ball buster for him."

"Could Zack have had something against Trey?" Jane suggested.

"Don't know how they would. They don't know each other, as far as I know," I said.

"Could Zack have known Trey from New York?" Rory asked.

Again, I shrugged. "I don't know. I didn't hang out in the same circles as Zack. He was always weary of the paranormal community, so our paths never really crossed apart from the classes we were in together."

"You could ask Grace," Jane suggested. "It would help clarify a few things."

I nodded. "Yeah, I'll see what I can do. Emily might know."

"I still don't understand," Bailey said. "Motive aside, what would a guy who doesn't jive with paranormals be doing in a place that deals in dark magic?"

"I don't know, but I doubt he was doing his laundry."

"Could he have followed us?" Jane asked.

"I doubt it," I said. "But if he somehow found out where we were going, I wouldn't put it past him to have come solely to get a head start on a story for the paper. My guess is he found out we were coming and made a point of getting to the guy first to interrogate him."

"Even if he found out we were coming to New York, though," Bailey said. "There's no way he would have been able to get the address of the building we were going to."

"My guess is he suckered Mrs. Brody into telling him," Jane said.

"She wouldn't have told him anything," Rory said.

I shrugged. "As much as it pains me to say, he's really good at what he does. He could have made her believe he was coming to help us or something."

"We need more information," Bailey sighed. "We need to know for sure why he came, and why the spell was bought in the first place.

I finished my coffee and pushed myself out of my seat. "Well, there's only one way to find out."

I took a few deep breaths to steady myself, then led the way across the street towards the laundromat. When we reached the front door, I turned back to face Bailey, Jane, and Rory, and attempted a confident smile. "I have no idea what we're going to find inside. If there's dark magic in there, it might be dangerous. I don't want to drag you guys into something that could possibly end badly."

Rory rolled her eyes. "If you think we're letting you go in there alone, you're crazy."

Bailey pushed passed me and opened the door. "Strength in numbers."

"Besides," Jane said as she followed Bailey into the building. "It's a laundromat. It's not like we're walking into some stranger's basement or anything."

I followed them inside, and allowed myself to relax as I took in the mundane surroundings. It was literally just a laundromat, complete with harsh fluorescent lights, loud machines that looked like they were installed in the 80's, two vending machines on the back wall, and a handful of grumpy-looking people listening to music and doing their laundry.

I laughed to myself as the nervous energy in my stomach dissipated.

I noticed a small desk in the back corner in front of a door that had a sign saying "office" hung crooked from a nail, and walked up to it and pressed the little bell.

I heard paper shuffling from behind the closed office door, but no one came. After a few more minutes I pressed the bell again. Still, nothing.

I sighed, and knocked loudly on the door.

"Excuse me," I shouted through the door. The sound of shuffling papers stopped, and then there was silence.

I sighed then knocked even harder on the door. The aggressive noise garnered a few looks from the laundry-doers in the room, but I ignored them. We had a growing list of questions, and I expected to get some answers.

When whoever was on the other side of the door still failed to answer, I attempted the door handle. As expected, it was locked. I glanced back at Bailey and she nodded, reading my mind. I stepped back from the door and with a snap of her fingers I heard the click from behind the door handle as the mechanism unlocked.

I grinned at Bailey who winked back at me. Sometimes it was fun being a witch.

I motioned for the girls to step back, then I pushed the office door open.

"Hey, what the…" a croaky voice said from inside the dark office. "That door was locked!"

We stepped into the office and were greeted by a greasy-looking thirty-something man in a Led Zeppelin t-shirt and baggy jeans hanging low, nearly to his knees.

"Do you work here?" I asked.

He kept looking back and forth between me and the door, his expression a mix of shock and confusion.

"She asked you a question," Bailey said after he didn't respond for at least a minute.

"I own this place." The man puffed out his chest. I didn't know if he was trying to look proud or if it was an attempt to look tough.

I rolled my eyes at him, and his expression turned to anger.

"Who are you?" he snapped at us.

"We're here to ask you a few questions," Rory said. She closed the door behind her as we all stepped further into his office.

He glanced nervously between the four of us, then returned his gaze to me.

"That doesn't answer my question," he said. "Who are you?"

"That doesn't matter," I said to him. "What matters is the reason we're here. Sit down."

He obeyed and sat down in his chair. He seemed to reconsider, though, and moved to stand back up a moment later.

"Sit," Bailey said, holding her hand straight out in front of her with her palm toward the man. He immediately shot back in his chair with force and looked up at her with wide, frightened eyes.

That seemed to get his attention. Good.

"What's your name?" Bailey asked. She continued holding her hand out toward the man. It didn't serve any purpose other than to frighten him, but the effect seemed to work wonders.

"Steve," he answered with a shaky voice.

"Steve," I repeated. "There was a guy in here about fifteen minutes ago. Green jacket, wearing a hood. What did he want?"

Steve shook his head frantically. "There was

nobody in here. I don't know what you're talking about."

"Liar," I spat at him. "We know he was here. We saw him leave."

Steve sunk back in his chair, seemingly completely deflated. Bailey lowered her arm, and the man rubbed his eyes. Poor guy seemed almost as tired as I felt.

After a few moments of contemplation, the man finally spoke. "Some journalist. Asked a bunch of questions. Complete nonsense. The guy was a lunatic."

I raised my eyebrow. "Oh? What kind of questions?"

Steve looked up at me with a pleading look in his eyes. I maintained my stern expression, and after a long minute of unbroken eye contact, Steve continued. "He asked if anyone had come to talk to me. I guess he was talking about you guys?"

I glared at him and waited for him to continue. When he didn't, I snapped my fingers and made a flame appear in my hand. His eyes went wide at the sight of the fire but kept his lips shut tight.

"Tell us what he said, or this fire in my hand will get a lot bigger," I threatened. "Truth or fire, your choice."

Steve whimpered, then thankfully decided to talk. I really didn't want to have to use that fire.

Besides, I probably wouldn't even know what to do with it even if I tried.

Steve looked up at me with a pleading look in his eye. "Please, don't make me talk. He said he would kill me if I talked."

I blinked in confusion. "What?"

"Please don't make me talk."

I looked to my side and Bailey and I exchanged worried looks. Rory and Jane were doing the same.

I finally looked back to Steve and resumed my stern expression, and after a long minute of unbroken eye contact, he continued. "He asked me about a murder and something to do with a cookie. Honestly, dude, I have no idea what he was going on about. Kept asking me what I knew."

I took a few steps forward so that I was looking straight down at the frightened-looking man in the chair. "Why was he asking you these questions?"

Steve shook his head. "I have no clue. Seriously, you have to believe me. He was just some whack job off the street."

"A journalist or a street person, which is it?" I glared at him.

He stared up at me unblinking. "Aw, man, I don't know. Believe me, please. Don't do anything... unnatural to me. Please."

I rolled my eyes and stepped back.

"Who else works here?" I asked. "Tell me the

names of everyone else who works in the laundromat."

Steve relaxed and pushed himself upright after slumping down in anxiety. "Just me. My last employee left a month ago, and I haven't been able to hire anyone since."

"So, you're saying you're the only one here, all day?" I glanced back at the girls. "So if someone were to come in, you would be the only one they would deal with, right?"

He nodded.

I ran my hand through my hair, trying to formulate my next question carefully. I stepped back and pushed myself up onto the desk and crossed my legs. If we had any hope of getting answers from this guy, he would have to feel comfortable enough to talk to us.

Following my lead, the girls stepped back and softened their expressions.

Once the atmosphere in the room lightened, I closed my eyes and put my feelers out to see if I could pick up any traces of magic. It was extremely faint, but it was there.

I opened my eyes and glanced to Bailey, who nodded back to me. Of course, she would be able to sense it. Looking to Jane and Rory, I could see that they picked up on it as well.

I turned back to Steve. "Tell us about the kind of magic you do."

He stared at me. "I don't know what you're talking about."

"Don't lie to me, Steve," I said, my voice gaining an edge of anger. "You don't want to make me angry. Bad things happen when I'm angry."

He swallowed, then shook his head. "I'm not lying. I don't do magic. Couldn't, even if I tried."

I narrowed my eyes at him. "There's magic in this room. I can sense it. We can all sense it."

His eyes darted across the room as if looking for something. After clearly not finding what he was looking for, he returned his gaze to me. "I don't... I don't have any idea what you're talking about."

"Did the guy ask about the spell?" I asked. I raised my arms as if to cast a spell, just to scare him a bit. I had no intention of casting anything.

"What spell?" Steve asked. He nearly broke down crying, barely managing to hold in tears. "Please, I don't know who he was or what he wanted. He just kept asking about a cookie. I have no idea what he was talking about. He didn't say anything about any sort of magic." He doubled over in his chair and placed his forehead in his hands, shaking his head back and forth.

I glanced to the girls who shrugged back. He seemed to be telling the truth.

"Not long ago you gave someone a spell capable of hurting people."

He snapped his head up at that and narrowed his

eyes at me. "It was you." I couldn't tell if that was a statement or a question.

Now, we were getting somewhere. "Who did you give that spell to?" I asked.

He paused then crossed his arms. "I don't know what you're talking about."

I sighed. "Bailey?"

"On it," Bailey answered. She rolled up her sleeves and raised her arms, and a slight wind picked up in the room. Steve's chair suddenly rolled back and slammed against the far wall from the force of Bailey's magic.

"Those are some nice clothes you're wearing," I commented. The fear was back in Steve's eyes. "Those shoes must have set you back, what, five hundred dollars?"

"Expensive taste for someone who runs a laundromat," Rory added.

I grinned as the poor guy grew increasingly uncomfortable. Rory rolled up her sleeves as well, and sheer panic spread across the man's face.

"Okay, okay," he said, raising his hands in surrender. "I'll talk."

Bailey lowered her hands and the wind in the room vanished.

"Thought so," I smiled. "First, you can tell me why we traced the spell to this establishment."

Steve sighed. "Fine. But keep it quiet from the

cops, okay? Promise me that, or else I won't tell you anything."

I nodded.

"Also, don't tell that guy who was just here that I told you anything, okay? I believed him when he said he's whack me off if I talked."

I nodded again.

"Fine. Not much money to be had in the laundry industry, as you can imagine," Steve began. "I sell stuff on the side. You know, drugs and that sort of shit. Every now and then, I have a customer ask for some kind of spell. Who am I to say no?" He offered a half smile, but quickly withdrew it as he saw we weren't smiling back.

"And someone came asking for a spell recently?" Rory asked.

Steve nodded. "Wanted something to temporarily stop a pulse. I've seen it in the movies and stuff. You know, the whole pretend to be dead so you can change your life thing, or something like that. The thing came in a vial—was some sort of potion or something. I don't really know much about that shit."

I gaped at him. "So, you sold someone a potion that would essentially kill them?"

He shook his head frantically. "Hell no, man. I'm not like that. Was just a trick spell, nothing serious. I don't even deal in the hard drugs. Mostly just weed and the occasional party pills."

"Who would want something like that?" Jane asked.

"Probably a criminal or something. Don't gotta go to jail if they think you're dead. You obviously don't watch much TV. One of the oldest tricks in the book." He laughed, but I was not amused. "Pretend to be dead, have a friend pick up your body, then, when the spell wears off, you're free to change your identity and live your life a free man."

"Where did you get the spell?" I demanded.

Steve shrugged. "I have a few sources. Friends of a friend, mostly. I dunno, man. As I said, I mostly just deal with other things."

I rubbed my eyes in aggravation. "What else?"

"They kept going on about cakes and shit. I told them to mix it into an entire cake. One bite would do the trick. There was enough for like twenty doses or something. I like to give my customers value, if you know what I mean. That's why they come back." I was disgusted with how proud he looked.

"Did you meet the person?"

"Nope. Talked on the phone, though. It was a woman. She wanted to stay anonymous. I'm assuming some kind of baker or something, the way she talked about the damn cakes. Do you guys know what a flan is? The lady wouldn't shut up about it."

I felt goosebumps appear on my arms and I glanced sideways to Rory, who looked back at me with a worried expression on her face. Mrs. Pots couldn't have done something like this, could she? Things really weren't looking good.

"So, what would happen if the spell was condensed into one serving?" I asked.

Steve laughed. "Oh, dude. Nothing good. Don't worry. I explained the instructions really clearly to the customer. They knew the risks."

I shook my head. How stupid could people be?

"Give me your wallet." I reached out my hand to him.

"What? No way, man."

"Do it," Bailey demanded. The wind in the room picked up again, and Steve scrambled to take his wallet out of his pocket and tossed it to me.

I pulled out his driver's license and snapped a picture of it with my phone.

"Steve Trevor Jameson." I placed his license back in the wallet and tossed it back to him.

"From now on you are out of the magic dealing business, got it?"

He swallowed hard but didn't respond.

"No more spells, or else we're going to the police," I said. "Understand?"

Steve nodded.

"Good. And if that guy comes back, we were never here." I looked from Bailey to Rory and Jane. "Anything else?"

They all shook their heads.

I turned my attention back to Steve. "If we find

out you're lying about not knowing the identity of your customer, you're going to find yourself in a hell of a lot of trouble, Steve Jameson."

Steve nodded quickly, his fear-filled eyes fixated on me.

"A *lot* of trouble," I repeated.

CHAPTER ELEVEN

Desperate to get home as soon as possible, we pretty much ran back to Emily's apartment to grab our things and said our goodbyes.

"Tell Grace we're going to get to the bottom of Trey's murder," I said as I hugged her goodbye. "Hopefully, we can help her get some closure."

Emily smiled. "I'll pass on the message next time I talk to her. I'm sure she'll be grateful for the effort you guys are putting into this."

"It's the least we can do." I gave her one last squeeze and then we headed out the door.

A few minutes later we were all packed in the car and on our way back out of the city.

"Well, that was a short and sweet," Bailey said.

"Maybe not so sweet," I countered.

I watched the city grow smaller as we drove

back north along the coast. It was a nice drive, and the weather had held up nicely.

"So, what are we going to do when we get back?" Rory asked. "You don't really think it was Mrs. Pots, do you guys?"

I sighed. "I'm not sure. I sure hope not."

"I mean, it could have just been a huge accident or misunderstanding. Maybe, Mrs. Pots had intended to use the spell for something else, and Trey just got caught in the middle of it?"

I shook my head. "I don't know. I really don't think Mrs. Pots is the kind of person to even meddle with that kind of magic. That woman doesn't have one vindictive bone in her body.

"Maybe she was trying to help someone out of a tough situation?" Jane offered.

We sat in silence for a while as Rory drove, and I pondered that idea for a while.

"Could be," I finally said. "It's out of character to use magic like that, but she does seem the type of person to go out of her way to help somebody out."

"We don't even know for sure that she's the one who bought the spell to begin with," Bailey said.

"Plus," Rory added. "We don't know what Zack said to the guy. For all we know, he could have planted information with the guy before we spoke to him."

I shook my head in disbelief. "I still can't believe

Zack was there. What the hell was he doing there? How did he know that's where we were headed?"

"Too many questions, not enough answers," Rory said.

"You've got that right."

We spent the rest of the car ride coming up with possible explanations for all of the weird things that had happened in the past few days, but we still didn't have any answers.

It was nearing five o'clock when we arrived back home. The drive was steady and there was barely any traffic, and we only had to stop for gas once.

Rory drove us directly to the station to visit Mrs. Pots. With any luck, she could help us set some things straight. The thought of her actually being responsible for Trey's murder made me sick to my stomach, and the idea of that kind, loving woman being sent to state prison was more than I could bare.

The station was quiet, and we waited a while in the front office before Sheriff Reese finally came to meet us.

"Here to see Mrs. Pots?" he asked as he walked up to the front desk.

I nodded. "Yeah, do you mind if we come in? We have some questions for Mrs. Pots."

"You and me, both," the Sheriff replied.

I raised my eyebrow, but he didn't add anything

to that statement. We followed him as he unlocked the back door and led us to the back room.

Mrs. Pots was standing in the back corner of his office painting invisible pictures on the wall with the eraser side of a pencil.

I suppressed a laugh. Mrs. Brody must not have reversed her spell when she left yesterday.

A broad smile was plastered across Mrs. Pots' face, and she was humming a tune as she worked away at her invisible art piece.

"She's been at that all day," Sheriff Reese said. He crossed his arms and shook his head as he watched her work. "Your landlady told us not to mind her, but I'm starting to worry that she's completely lost her mind."

Rory laughed. "Who, Mrs. Pots or Mrs. Brody?"

Sheriff Reese looked at her and nodded. "Both, I suppose."

I sat down on the couch against the side wall of the office. "Mrs. Pots, do you mind if we talk?"

The short, portly woman turned towards me and spread her arms out as if to give me a hug from across the room. "Oh, River, dear. What a lovely surprise. I didn't even hear you come in."

I grinned. "Would you like to join me on the couch, Mrs. Pots? I have some questions for you."

I don't know what Mrs. Brody did to her, but I was thankful that she at least seemed to be enjoying herself. You would assume that being held in a precinct as a murder suspect would be a stressful situation. She's not locked behind bars, though, so, my guess is that the Sheriff knows just as well as we do that she's innocent. They just have to hold her here under protocol until we can find proof against the claim that she's responsible for Trey's death.

Mrs. Pots came to join me on the couch and set down her pencil carefully on the side table before turning to look expectantly at me.

"Would you like a cookie, dear?" she asked me.

"Er, no, thank you, Mrs. Pots," I answered. "I have some questions for you about what happened on Halloween. You do remember why you're here, right?" I had no idea what sort of effect this spell had on her, but I hoped it didn't interfere with her memory.

"Of course, dear," she said. "I remember it perfectly."

I nodded. "I'm sure you're getting tired of recounting the same story to everybody, but do you mind telling me everything you remember from the party?"

"My pleasure, sweetheart." Mrs. Pots stood and stepped away from the couch. She then turned to everyone in the room and spread her arms out dramatically as she prepared herself for what looked like was going to be a dramatic reenactment of Halloween night.

"It was just before midnight, and the young man and who planned to steal my business came to talk to me at the dessert table."

I rubbed my eyes. "You know, you're really not helping your case by saying things like that, Mrs. Pots."

She waved her hand at me in disregard. "Oh, nonsense." She then cleared her throat before continuing. "He was actually quite lovely and was explaining how he was planning on settling down here, maybe starting a family with Grace. He was ever so enthusiastic about my cookies, which was very flattering."

"We all love your cookies," Sheriff Reese said. He pulled up a chair next to the couch and took a seat.

"I know, dear," Mrs. Pots said. "You really should cut back, though. It's starting to show around the middle, if you know what I mean."

I did my best to suppress a laugh, but it sneaked out anyways. Sheriff Reese blushed and did not look impressed. I pretended to ignore him and looked intently up to Mrs. Pots. "What happened next?"

"I offered him my new pumpkin butter cookie," she said. "He took a bite and... well, you know the rest."

"I'd prefer if you told it to the end," Sheriff Reese said.

She sighed and her eyes filled with sadness.

"The poor boy fell to the ground, and that was it. Didn't even seem to choke or show any sign of struggle. He just... fell."

Sheriff Reese turned to me and frowned. "Like I said before, the lab found no trace of poison. The autopsy revealed no sign of respiratory struggle, though, either. It appears he didn't choke, so, I'm inclined to believe your hypothesis about something supernatural being involved."

"It's not simply a hypothesis," I told him. "There's no doubt that the cookie was spelled with dark magic. The only thing we don't know is if it was an accident or intentional, and if it was intentional, who did it and why."

Sheriff Reese nodded. "Exactly. You realize, being the only witches in town, this doesn't bode well for you and your house?"

I raised my eyebrow. "We were the ones to tell you about the spell. If we had anything to do with this, which is absolutely ridiculous, why would we have told you the cookie was spelled in the first place?"

The Sheriff nodded and rubbed his eyes. "I know. It's just we have nothing else to go on, and I'm at a complete loss when it comes to this sort of thing."

"We'll help in any way that we can," I said.

We all sat in silence for a few minutes, lost in our own thoughts.

A knock came from the front room and Sheriff Reese excused himself.

I looked up to my housemates, who looked just as defeated as I felt.

"Mrs. Pots, have you been to New York recently?" I asked her when I was sure Sheriff Reese was out of ear shot.

"My dear, I haven't left Brimstone Bay in decades. Why do you ask?"

"It's just that we traced the spell that killed Trey back to a location in New York. We managed to find the person who sold it."

Mrs. Pots blinked. "Did you find anything?"

I shook my head, not wanting to share every detail of what we learned. It was probably best to keep the part of the buyer likely being a baker a secret until we know more. "Just that someone purchased the spell knowing full well the effect it would have on the victim."

"I see." Mrs. Pots nodded thoughtfully. "But how did it get in my cookie?"

I sighed. "I don't know, Mrs. Pots. Are you absolutely sure you don't know anything more about this? Anything that could help us find out who did this?"

Mrs. Pots shook her head. "No, I honestly have no idea. No one had access to anything I baked until I put them out on the table on Sunday. But I guess anyone could have done something then?"

I turned back to the girls. "Sounds like it was likely someone at the party."

"I honestly can't think of anyone in Brimstone Bay who would do something like this. Especially, to someone new to town," Rory said.

"What if it was just an accident?" Bailey asked.

I shrugged. "That idea worries me more than if Trey were murdered."

"What do you mean?" Rory asked, joining me on the couch.

"Well," I began. "If it was an accident, then that means a toxic spell somehow found its way into Mrs. Pots' cookies without anyone knowing. If that's the case, then we're all at risk of being poisoned or, worse, killed."

"Oh, no, no, no," Mrs. Pots said, holding her hands against her cheeks and shaking her head back and forth dramatically. "My baking. You mean my baking is all at risk? My baking could kill more people?"

"We didn't sense any magic in any of the other items on Mrs. Pots' table when we searched, remember?" Jane said.

I nodded. "Right, which makes me think that it was definitely intentional."

"Besides, who would go to the trouble of sourcing a dark magic spell all the way from New York if not for a specific purpose?"

"That makes sense," Bailey said.

"What makes sense?" Mayor Scott said as he followed Sheriff Reese back into the office.

"Hey, Mayor Scott," I said, smiling up at the Mayor as he took a seat on the edge of the desk across the room.

He nodded to me. "What makes sense?" he repeated.

"We were just saying how we think the act was intentional," I said. "The spell was isolated to that one cookie. It was definitely meant to harm somebody. Whether Trey was the target, I'm not sure."

The Mayor rubbed his chin in thought. "I see. And Mrs. Pots was the one who gave the cookie to Trey?"

Mrs. Pots nodded. "Yes, that was me."

"We've been over this," I said. I stood and began pacing the room. "She had no idea the cookie was poisoned. Someone must have planted it there in the hopes that it would be eaten."

"Anyone could have eaten it, though," Mayor Scott said.

I nodded. "In theory, yes."

"We'll have to assume it was intended for Trey for now. That way we can keep our investigation focused. If we learn anything that suggests otherwise, we will act accordingly. Until then, we're searching for anything that will help lead us to the person responsible for the murder."

"We'll do our best to assist in the investigation," I said to Sheriff Reese.

The Sheriff nodded and rubbed his chin. "We need to get to the bottom of this, fast. The state police are responsible for murder investigations, and if we can't prove Mrs. Pots' innocence, then I'm afraid they'll be taking over sooner than we anticipate."

"Who else was near Trey when it happened?" Mayor Scott answered.

"Grace, his wife," I said.

"Statistically, it's often the spouse," Sheriff Reese said. "We'll certainly have to bring her in for questioning. Does anyone have any reason to believe she was involved?"

I shook my head. "They're planning on starting a family. Or they were, in any case."

"She was absolutely hysterical when it happened," Bailey said. "I can't imagine she could have made that up."

"Besides, it doesn't make sense to kill your business partner when he's the one responsible for the success of the business," I added, trying to think pragmatically. "I really don't think there's any way she could have done it."

"I agree with you," Sheriff Reese said. "Besides, it wouldn't have made sense for her to do it so publicly. There are much more discreet ways to murder a spouse."

I rolled my eyes. "Could we not talk about this, right now? It's getting a little morbid, and Grace is my friend. She needs support right now, not a bunch of people talking about her behind her back."

"You're right," Mayor Scott said. "We need to focus our attentions on finding the real killer. If the state finds out we're holding a potential suspect here, they'll want to take her away to their own facilities."

Mrs. Pots had resumed her humming and seemed lost again in her thoughts.

"Can you ask Mrs. Brody to fix this?" Sheriff Reese motioned to Mrs. Pots. "I can't leave her alone if she's spelled like a child."

I sighed. "Yes, we'll ask her once we get home."

I grinned to Mrs. Pots, who winked back when the Sheriff had turned his back.

Sheriff Reese nodded. "Thank you. I think it's best you all leave now. We've got a lot of work to do, and only so much time before the Feds step in and take over the investigation."

"How long do we have?" I asked.

"I'd say no more than a few days. We need to think quickly if we're going to keep Mrs. Pots out of jail. The Feds won't be so lenient with a first-hand eye witness to the murder."

"Too bad we have no leads and no idea how to

solve this thing," I said glumly as we made our way out through the front office.

We left feeling completely defeated and hopeless, with no new insights or even a glimpse of hope.

CHAPTER TWELVE

WE HAD BARELY PULLED OUT OF THE POLICE STATION
parking lot when I nearly jumped out of my seat.

"Oh, my God, why didn't I think of this earlier?"
I shouted.

The girls all stared at me and waited for me to
continue.

"His ghost," I said. "Why didn't we think of this
before? Why don't we just ask his ghost?"

Jane laughed. "We did just go through this a few
weeks ago. I can't believe we missed something so
obvious."

I laughed as well. "I know, right? Could have
saved us the entire trip to New York."

"And we know exactly where his ghost would
be," Rory said. "We don't even have to send out a
search party."

"It's so obvious," I said. "Trey was standing

there talking to Mrs. Pots for at least twenty minutes before it happened. If anyone would have seen someone lurking around the dessert table, it would have been him."

We drove the rest of the way home with a newfound confidence and a solid game plan.

Rory had barely put the car in park when I bounded out the door and raced around the house into the backyard. Mrs. Brody was busy taking down the decorative lights toward the rear of the yard near the bluffs, and I ran to join her.

"Whoa, calm yourself," Mrs. Brody said to me as I tried talking through winded breaths. I tried to remember the last time I had gone for a run around the boardwalk, and realized it must have been nearly a month. No wonder I was so out of shape.

I took a few deep breaths to regain my composure, and, by the time I could speak clearly, the girls had joined us in the yard.

"His ghost," I finally managed to say. "Trey's ghost. Why don't we just ask him what happened? He probably knows more about what happened than any of us do."

Mrs. Brody thought about that for a moment, then smiled. "Well, of course. What a great idea."

She dropped what she was doing and led us back towards the house.

"How long does it typically take a ghost to appear after their murder?" I asked.

"Oh, it's uncertain," she replied. "Whenever they're ready, I imagine."

The table where Mrs. Pots had set out her desserts was right near the back of the house, and was still cordoned off with police tape.

"He would appear right here, wouldn't he?" Bailey asked.

I nodded. "From what I learned during the Shadow Festival the other week, ghosts typically appear at the site of their murder. It's not a hard and fast rule; if you remember, Jessica and Mr. and Mrs. Littleton's ghosts appeared here in town rather than at the site of their murders."

We looked around the table and the rest of the yard, but saw no sign of Trey's ghost.

"That's not to say they didn't appear there first," Mrs. Brody offered. "We can ask the experts, though."

After a minute of silence, Mrs. Brody spoke again. "Oh, we all know you're lurking about, Mr. Richardson. You might as well make yourself useful."

Without hesitation, Mr. Richardson's spirit arrived through the living room wall.

"You rang, my dear?" he bowed to Mrs. Brody.

She rolled her eyes. "You know, you really should find your own place to live. You can't keep loitering in my apartment, pretending not to be here."

"I don't loiter," Mr. Richardson turned up his nose.

"Poltergeist," Mrs. Brody accused.

"Old hag," Mr. Richardson rebutted.

"Okay, children," I interrupted. "Play time is over. Time to mingle with the grownups."

Mrs. Brody rolled her eyesand went to busy herself in the kitchen nearby.

"Mr. Richardson, how long does it take for a person's ghost to appear after they die?"

"Not all people return as ghosts, my dear."

I nodded. "I remember. Only murder victims, right?"

"Correct," he said. "It never takes long. A person's spirit technically appears immediately. Sometimes, it takes them a while to accept their death and materialize as an entity, however."

"So, you're saying Trey's ghost should, in theory, be here already?"

"Trey's ghost?" the spirit raised his eyebrow. "Are you telling me a murder occurred here?"

"Oh, don't play dumb," Mrs. Brody snapped at him. "You know everything that goes on in this place, you translucent nosy pervert."

"Well, I say," Mr. Richardson held his hand to his chest and feigned insult. "I resemble that remark."

Mr. Richardson winked at me, and I couldn't help but grin.

"Besides, I've got better things to do with my time than watch *you* all the time, Mrs. Brody."

He put an emphasis on the word 'you,' and my grin quickly turned into a frown.

"Are you implying…" I began, but he quickly interrupted me.

"To answer your question," the ghost said. "There is no reason why your spirit should not be here by now. All you need to do is find him. I can help if you like."

"His ghost can wait," I said sharply. "I'd like to clarify something first, if you don't mind." I put my hands on the hips and looked at Mr. Richardson expectantly.

"Oh, my, look at the time," the spirit glanced down at his watch-less wrist. "Things to do, people to see."

With that, Mr. Richardson turned and disappeared through the exterior wall.

I glared after him. "You don't think he watches us upstairs, do you?"

Mrs. Brody shrugged. "Oh, who knows what any of those old farts are up to when we're not looking."

I blinked, confused. "Okay, I'm really weirded out right now."

Rory was holding her arms across her chest and looked rather pale. "They can't see us in the shower, can they?"

Mrs. Brody patted her on the shoulder then laughed. "Oh, I wouldn't worry about that, dear."

"So, no?" Rory tried to confirm.

"I just wouldn't worry about that."

We all eyed each other, then looked back to Mrs. Brody.

"That's not really an answer," I said.

"Don't you have a murder to solve?" she asked.

I sighed. "Yes. Fine." I then raised my voice and shouted to the walls. "But don't think this is over!"

I shuddered, then tried to push the thought of peeping tom old man ghosts from my mind.

"Shall we go find Trey?" Rory asked.

"Sounds like a plan." The girls left the apartment and headed towards the backyard.

"Is there anything we can do to encourage his ghost to appear?" I asked Mrs. Brody.

She nodded to me, then walked over to her large cabinet next to the counter. She pulled out a large metal container with a tight-fitting lid and removed a handful of large, dried and shriveled leaves.

"Tobacco," she said. "Among other things."

"Really?" I asked, skeptical. "How does that help?"

Mrs. Brody rolled a number of leaves together and tied it with string. "It's nourishment for the spirits. The ritual dates back to cultures who were along long before we arrived on this continent. It's very powerful stuff."

"So, we just burn it?"

She nodded. "Try not to breathe too much in, if you can help it."

I laughed and rolled my eyes. "Just what we need, a bunch of stoned witches summoning spirits."

Mrs. Brody handed me the wrapped leaves and wished me luck. I hesitantly took it from her and joined the girls outside.

"What's that?" Rory asked.

"Is that tobacco?" Jane walked up to the bundle in my hand and smelled. "Yep."

"Tobacco and something," I added. "Not too sure what the 'something' is, though."

"Oh, smart," Bailey reached over to take the tobacco from me, and I eagerly handed it to her. "I've read about ancient rituals using tobacco to summon spirits."

"It's all yours," I said. "Besides, we don't really need to summon him. We just need to find him."

Bailey smiled. "Either way, this will help."

"Just don't get me too stoned," I said. "I'd like to keep my head relatively clear for when we ask him questions."

"Relax, it's just tobacco," Bailey said.

"Just tobacco," I laughed.

"And something," Rory added.

"And something," Jane repeated.

I rolled my eyes.

Bailey walked over to a torch that was still

burning in the yard and lit the end of the bundle. She then waved out the flame and a steady stream of smoke emanated from the tips of the leaves.

"That doesn't actually smell that bad," I commented.

Bailey smiled. "That's the tobacco talking." She winked at me then proceeded to wave the smoke over the area surrounding the table.

We all stood in silence and watched.

After a few awkward minutes of standing around, I was starting to become dizzy. "Okay, I think that's enough with the *tobacco,* I think."

"Are we doing it right?" Rory asked. "Should we be chanting anything? Is there a way for us to call him?"

I shrugged. "I don't know, but we're not doing ourselves any good breathing in all this smoke. If I breathe in any more of this stuff, I'll be seeing spirits that aren't actually here." I coughed and had to sit down on the grass to prevent myself from falling down as my head felt like it was spinning a mile a minute.

Bailey extinguished the bundle and joined me on the grass.

"So, now what?" she asked.

"We wait?" I suggested. "Don't really know what else we can do. Trey's ghost is our only hope of figuring this whole thing out."

"What if he didn't see anything?" Bailey asked. "What do we do then?"

I rubbed my eyes. "I don't know. It's not looking good for Mrs. Pots."

Bailey sighed. "You don't think she actually did it, do you?"

"I don't know what I think anymore."

Mrs. Brody came to join us in the backyard a while later, carrying a tray of tea. She set it down on a table and joined Bailey and me on the grass. I reached for a mug of the steaming tea and smiled as I breathed in the relaxing smell of the chamomile tea.

I was a coffee drinker through and through, but there was nothing like a cup of tea to calm the soul.

"Any luck?" Mrs. Brody asked.

I shook my head. "No, nothing. I'm not sure what else we can do."

"There's nothing you can do but wait, I'm afraid."

"Oh, I forgot to mention," I said while I still remembered. "Sheriff Reese asked if you could reverse whatever spell you cast on Mrs. Pots. I smirked at my landlady as she sipped her tea innocently, averting my gaze.

She finally shrugged. "I reversed it when I left."

I narrowed my eyes at her. "Mrs. Brody, she was painting the walls with an eraser and was humming the soundtrack to cats."

Mrs. Brody laughed. "Oh, smart woman, she's probably milking it for all it's worth."

"So, she's really not under a spell?" Bailey asked.

"That was one hundred percent Nancy Pots," Mrs. Brody laughed. "She probably knows the Sheriff won't lock her up if she's still under my influence."

I shook my head. "Clever."

Another twenty minutes passed, and I fell back against the grass and stared up at the cloudy sky. At what point do we just give up?

"Bored?" Mr. Richardson appeared out of nowhere in the backyard and came to float next to the dessert table.

I had nearly fallen asleep. "It's no hope. Trey's ghost doesn't seem to want to show up."

Mr. Richardson shrugged. "Maybe he didn't realize he was murdered."

I sat upright and stared at him. "What do you mean? I thought you said all murder victims come back as ghosts?"

"They do," the ghost said. "But his spirit could have been confused. Perhaps he thought he simply choked."

I shook my head. "I don't understand. How does that make any sense? You get to choose whether you come back or not?"

Mr. Richardson paused. "Well, no, not exactly."

I fell back on the grass and rubbed my eyes. "I don't understand."

"I'm simply suggesting that perhaps his spirit was convinced he wasn't murdered, and passed on."

"In order for that to happen, then he obviously wouldn't have witnessed anything suspicious before dying, right?'

"Correct."

I sighed. "So that at least confirms that whoever spelled the cookie did so without Trey seeing anything."

"Does that help in your investigation at all, dear?" Mrs. Brody asked.

I stared up at the clouds passing by overhead and thought for a moment. "Yes, I think so. We know that the cookie was either spelled before Trey approached Mrs. Pots' table, or else it was done in such a way that he didn't suspect anything wrong."

Well, at least that was something.

My phone rang in my pocket a moment later, and Sheriff Reese's name flashed across my screen.

I answered on speaker phone and held the phone out for everyone to hear.

"You're on speaker," I said to the Sheriff.

"River," Sheriff Reese sounded serious. "Bad news."

I sat bolt upright. "Tell me."

"Just got a call from the higher-ups. They're coming tonight to transfer Mrs. Pots to a state

163

facility. After ten o'clock, this will be out of our hands."

I hung up the phone and fell back on the ground in silence.

If we didn't solve this case in the next few hours, Mrs. Pots would end up in prison.

Great.

CHAPTER THIRTEEN

I HAD TOTALLY FORGOTTEN THAT JORDAN AND I HAD rescheduled our dinner date for that night.

It was a good thing, actually, as I would have probably been nervous all day and that really wouldn't have helped the day go by any easier. It seemed a bad time, and I considered rescheduling again, but it would be a nice distraction from the stresses of the day.

We originally agreed to go to a new French restaurant in a small bed and breakfast just outside of town, but there was a mix up with the reservation or something, so, we decided to go to the local sports bar instead.

I rummaged through the pile of clothes I had strewn across my bed, but couldn't seem to find anything appropriate to wear. The first outfit I tried on felt too fancy, so I switched it out for my favorite pair of ripped jeans and a t-shirt, but then that felt too casual.

I kicked off the jeans and pulled on a pair of black high-waisted skinnies, but couldn't find a top to go with it.

I was ready to pull my hair out when I heard a knock from my door and Rory poked her head in my room.

"You sound like you're having a fight with the cats," she said, laughing from just outside of my bedroom. "Need help finding something to wear?"

My frustration must have manifested itself in grunting noises, as she also claimed she heard a buffalo coming from my room.

I rolled my eyes, but accepted the offer graciously.

"I hate this," I said. "It's just a date. I don't know why I'm so nervous."

Rory came to my bed and helped sort through the massive pile of clothes.

"You must really like the guy," she said. "It's normal."

I grunted, then turned my attention back to the clothes.

"I've got nothing to wear."

"Those pants look great," Rory said. "Pair that with your back boots and you're good to go."

"And what? Just show up wearing my bra as a shirt?"

She laughed. "I've got just the thing. Hang on."

Rory raced out of my room and up the stairs. I continued to rummage through the clothes, but gave up after a moment and sat down on the foot of my bed, defeated.

"If I can't even dress myself, what hope do I have of managing a relationship?" I asked Soot as he jumped up to join me on the bed.

My little gray cat rolled over on his back for belly rubs as he always liked to do, and I obliged. I welcomed the distraction.

"Here," Rory announced as she came back into the room.

She was holding up a long, light-gray sweater.

"Oh, cute," I said. Rory tossed it to me, and I slid it on over my head, then went to look at myself in the mirror. "Perfect!"

The sweater fit snug and had a wide neckline that showed off my shoulders. It was nice, yet casual, and would pair perfectly with my black boots.

"It's Bailey's," Rory said. "She's too busy chatting with that bartender from New York. I haven't seen that girl so love-struck since she first met Ryan Bramley."

I laughed. "Good. She needed someone new to help her get over that creep. A new guy is just the distraction she needs."

"Too bad he lives in New York."

I shrugged. "It's not that far. Maybe this means we'll have more road trips coming up."

I turned and posed in front of Rory like a mannequin.

"Thoughts?"

"You look great," Rory said, beaming at me. "Just don't embarrass yourself by spilling anything on it, or falling in those boots of yours." She winked at me.

I laughed. "Oh, you know I'll screw something up."

I checked my phone and saw that I only had fifteen minutes before I was supposed to meet Jordan.

"Crap, I gotta go." I grabbed my bag and kissed Rory on the cheek on my way out. "Don't wait up."

For the sake of time, I rode my bike into town. Luckily, the clouds had cleared and it didn't look like it was going to rain.

I locked my bike up in front of work and noticed JoAnn pacing in the window of our office. She had her arms folded behind her head, and she looked upset.

I still had five minutes before I had to meet Jordan, and my conscience insisted I go up and see what was going on. "Dammit," I muttered to myself as I climbed the stairs.

JoAnn was alone in the office and continued to pace as I opened the door and came in.

"Everything okay, JoAnn?" I asked.

JoAnn jumped as my voice startled her and she stopped pacing.

"Oh, hey, River," she said. "What are you doing here?"

"Was just on my way to dinner and I saw you through the window. Are you okay?"

JoAnn sighed and sat down at her desk. "Yes, I'm fine. Just dealing with some personal things." Her eyes flicked to Zack's desk, and I could guess who she was referring to.

I didn't ask for details. Not only was it none of my business, but I really didn't want to know.

"Anything I can do?" I asked.

She shook her head. "That's sweet of you, but no. I'm okay. You go enjoy your dinner."

"Will do," I said. I tried to give her my warmest smile, but she was preoccupied staring out the window, lost again in her own thoughts.

I walked over to her and squeezed her shoulder. "Things will work out. Try and enjoy the rest of your night."

JoAnn smiled at me and took my hand in hers. "You're doing a good job, River."

That took me by surprise, and I paused for a minute.

JoAnn was a very kind person, and I even considered her a friend of sorts, but when it came to work, she rarely gave out compliments. She never hesitated to rip our work apart or request changes we would have to make on our articles. She had really high standards of work and expected us to submit topnotch work every time.

This was the first time I think she's ever complimented me on my work. The poor woman must really be rattled.

"Thank you, JoAnn."

I scanned the office before leaving, to see if I could find any clue as to how Zack would have found out the address we had visited in New York. I thought maybe I had left my laptop in the office or something, but that didn't appear to be the case. The only way I could think of for him to have gotten that address would have been for him to hack into my computer account or something. Zack was a competitive asshole, but even that seemed a stretch for him.

"I'll see you tomorrow," I said as I left her alone in the office. I really hoped she'd sort out whatever issues she was going through. A depressed editor meant a very challenging workday.

I checked my phone and realized I was running a few minutes late, and jogged the rest of the way to Joe's Sports Bar.

Joe's was really more of a bar, and that definition was even a stretch. It closer resembled a small restaurant with a bar and a few tables on the main floor of one of the old houses on the main strip in town. They claimed to have the best nachos in town, which I believed as they were probably the only place in town you could actually get nachos.

Jordan was waiting for me in front of the bar, and greeted me with a hug when I arrived.

"Hey," I said as he released me from the hug. "Sorry if I'm late."

"Not late at all," he said. "Shall we?" He motioned towards the front door, and I led the way inside.

We were the only ones in the place, apart from one server who, I suspected, was also the kitchen staff as he was wearing both waiter's apron and chef's hat.

We chose a table in front of the fireplace away from the TVs and ordered a couple of drinks.

"So, tell me about New York," Jordan said. "I want to hear all about it." The sound of TVs buzzed in the background, and I turned my chair so I wasn't watching whatever sports news show was on.

Ignoring the TVs, I smiled at him. His blue eyes lit up when he talked to me, and it made my heart melt. Just a little bit.

"It was short," I answered. "We didn't really get up to much. Just visited a friend and went for a few drinks."

"River," Jordan narrowed his eyes at me.

I paused. "Yes?"

"We both know that you didn't just go down

there to see a friend. What were you guys doing in New York?"

Damn, I sometimes forget that he's an ex-cop. "Can't hide anything from you, can I?" I laughed.

Jordan laughed and shook his head. "Not even worth trying."

I sighed, then looked around to make sure no one could hear me. The waiter had dropped off our drinks and went back to the kitchen, so I assumed I was safe to talk.

"The girls and I managed to trace the spell that killed Trey back to New York City. We went to investigate."

Jordan stared at me and I noticed a slight flush appear on his cheeks. "River, what did I tell you about getting involved?"

I rolled my eyes. "I appreciate the concern, but I didn't really have a choice. If we don't find out who is responsible for Trey's death, then Mrs. Pots may spend the rest of her life in prison for manslaughter."

Jordan sat back in his chair and sipped his beer. "How do we know that she isn't actually responsible? All evidence points to her, and if there's anything I learned from my time in the force, it's that you really never know a person. No matter how close you think you are to them."

I sighed. "I know without a doubt that she's not the murderer. She doesn't have one bad bone in her body."

"I heard her say, with my own ears, that she wished Trey and Grace would just disappear." He slammed his glass down on the table with force and I jumped at the loud noise it made. "Everyone knows she wasn't happy about our dessert shop opening up across the street from her bakery. She had every reason to want Trey gone."

Okay, now I was starting to get a mad. "Jordan, you don't know her. She wouldn't hurt a fly. I promise you, there is absolutely no way that she did this." The anger was starting to show in my voice, and I crossed my arms when I finished talking. He had no business moving to town and accusing one of our own of murder, and I was starting to second guess my decision in going on a date with him.

Jordan obviously caught on to my change in attitude and reached across the table for my hand. Reluctantly, I uncrossed my arms and placed my hand in his.

He squeezed his eyes shut and took a deep breath. "You're right," he said. "We really don't know what happened. Maybe I'm letting my emotions get the better of me."

Right, I forgot Trey was Jordan's close friend.

"I'm so sorry about your friend, Jordan," I said as I gave his hand a squeeze. "This can't be easy for you."

He shook his head. "Whenever I begin to feel

sorry for myself, I just think of Grace. I have no business being sad when she just lost her husband."

"I don't think it works that way, but it's kind of you to be thinking of her," I said. "Have you heard from her at all?"

He shook his head. "Not yet, I'm letting her have her space for now. So, tell me more about New York. Did your investigation lead to anything?"

"Yeah, actually," I said. I figured there was no sense in keeping secrets from him. As an ex-cop, he might even be able to help us make sense out of everything. "We found the guy who sold the spell that poisoned the cookie."

Jordan nearly jumped out of his chair. "Are you serious? Did you call the police?"

I shook my head. "No. He was just some dumb low-life drug dealer."

"River," Jordan was rubbing his eyes. I could tell he was preparing for another one of his lectures.

"It's done, Jordan," I said. "No sense stressing out over it, now."

This date was really taking a turn for the worse.

"What did he say?" he managed to finally say after taking a few calming breaths. At least, he was making an attempt to be supportive. Once a cop, always a cop.

"Well, we know the person who bought the spell was a woman."

Jordan nodded. "Okay."

"They also apparently mentioned baking quite a bit, and we suspect the person might have been a baker."

A knot formed in my stomach as I heard myself say those words.

"Okay," Jordan repeated. "You realize this doesn't look good for Mrs. Pots."

"I know."

"Have you told Sheriff Reese about any of this?"

I shook my head. "No, I haven't."

The waiter couldn't have chosen a better time to come take our order. It saved me from having to take any flak from Jordan for not reporting everything I knew to Sheriff Reese.

"There's something else," I said.

Jordan cocked an eyebrow and waited for me to continue.

"Zack Brendon was there."

"Who?"

"The other journalist at work. The one JoAnn hired a few weeks ago."

Jordan sat up straighter and fixed his eyes on me. "He was in New York?"

"We saw him leave the place where the drug dealer was." I paused, the memory making me feel uneasy. "They spoke, Jordan."

"You should have led with that part," he said. "Did you speak to him?"

I shook my head. "No. He left before we went in."

"Do you think he's involved?" Jordan asked. "Why would he have been there?"

"I don't know," I answered. "But he seemed to be interested if we had questioned the guy."

Jordan pushed his chair back and looked as if he were about to stand. "Classic signs of someone trying to cover up a trail. River, it really looks to me like this guy had something to do with the murder."

"Or he was just trying to beat me to the story," I offered. "It's not out of character for him to do something this drastic just to advance his career."

"I don't know, River." Jordan was shaking his head. "This doesn't look good. We need to report this to the sheriff."

"The guy said the person who ordered the spell was a woman, though, remember?" I said. "And I can't stop thinking about the whole baking thing. I just can't bring myself to believe any of this."

"I know it's hard," Jordan said. "But the best we can do right now is just offer as much information as we can to Sheriff Reese, and let him take it from there."

I sighed. "Maybe you're right. I think I've been mildly in shock since the night of the murder. I'm having trouble making sense of anything. Maybe I'm not thinking straight."

Jordan reached out and took my hands in his.

"It's not your responsibility to solve this, you know. We'll go to the station together after we eat, and Sheriff Reese can take it from here. Okay?"

I stared at him then nodded a moment later. "I guess you're right."

"For now, let's just enjoy the evening, okay?"

"Yeah, okay. I'm just having trouble wrapping my mind around the idea that Zack might have killed Trey. It just doesn't make sense."

The giant tray of nachos finally arrived, and the waiter brought us two new beers to replace our empty glasses. "These ones are on the house," he said, then winked at me.

I raised my eyebrows as he walked away. "Wow, they must really be grateful for our business."

Jordan laughed. "I'm guessing they don't get many people in here on weekdays?"

"Or any day, really," I added.

We ate in silence for a few minutes, and I tried to push the stresses of my day out of my mind. That was until the TV caught my attention and I nearly choked.

"Is that Grace?" I asked.

Jordan turned to look at the TV, and his mouth fell open. "Sure is."

I called for the waiter to turn the volume up so we could listen.

The channel was set to an international news

station, and the anchor was interviewing Grace in front of the Coliseum in Rome.

"Is she in Italy?" Jordan asked.

I nodded. "Yeah. What is she doing on TV?"

Jordan shook his head and stared up at the television. "She looks surprisingly good."

The text at the bottom of the screen read, "Desserti Comes to Rome."

"The announcement that the popular American dessert restaurant chain, Desserti, is coming to Rome has caused quite the stir in the local culinary community," the anchor was saying through the television. "We are joined today with the new full owner of the popular chain, Grace Wong."

I turned back to Jordan. "Did you know about this?"

Jordan shook his head. "Trey never mentioned it. In fact, he told me he was hoping to sell every restaurant apart from the New York City one and this new one in town."

"That certainly doesn't seem to be what's happening now," I said.

Grace was absolutely radiant on the television; a wide smile spread across her face as she spoke to the anchor.

"I am so pleased to announce that Desserti is going global. We've just signed contracts in five major international cities, in addition to the nine new restaurants we will be opening up in the United States."

"Absolutely remarkable," the anchor spoke directly to the camera. "And this is all happening after the devastating loss of her husband not two days ago."

The anchor turned back to Grace. "Grace, how are you handling all of this while dealing with so much grief?"

Grace wiped a tear from her eye as she took the microphone from her interviewer. "It is indeed a tragic time for all of us, but the one thing keeping me going through all of this is the fact that I know Trey is watching over us all throughout the duration of this expansion with a big, proud smile on his face. This expansion was Trey's ultimate dream, and I know he would be so proud of the entire Desserti team. I know my husband is looking down at me right now."

Grace put her hand on her heart and looked up to the ceiling above her as tears welled down her face. "Trey, baby, this is for you."

The scene cut from the interview to a montage of photos of the Desserti restaurant chain.

I slowly turned to look at Jordan. His face was beat red, and his glass was on the verge of exploding under his iron grip. He was shaking his head back and forth and muttering something along the lines of, "That lying bitch," under his breath.

"Jordan," I managed to say after trying to find my voice.

I paused as he turned to look at me. "A baker. The woman who bought the spell was a baker."

He raised his eyebrow, clearly not following my train of thought.

"The woman who bought the spell from that guy in New York," I repeated. "She baked cakes. She told the guy that she made cakes."

Finally, he clued in. "You don't think…"

He turned to look back at the TV, which was still showing pictures of the restaurant. A smiling picture of Trey and Grace popped up on the screen, and Jordan's glass finally shattered under the pressure of his grip.

We both spoke at once. "It was Grace."

CHAPTER FOURTEEN

JORDAN THREW SOME CASH ON THE TABLE AND WE ran out of the restaurant together towards Jordan's car. We had to get to the police station before the state police arrived and took Mrs. Pots away.

"How are we going to prove this?" I asked as Jordan drove us to the station.

"I don't know, but we can start with explaining everything from the beginning." He was practically seething, and I realized I probably should have offered to drive.

The poor guy just discovered that one of his closest friends was murdered by his own wife. I wouldn't imagine what must have been going through his head at that moment.

Jordan pulled us into the station, and we ran inside to find the front office full of people in uniform. Sheriff Reese was behind the desk with his eyes closed, rubbing his temples, and looking particularly stressed out.

"What's going on here?" I asked.

The officers around us ignored me. I coughed, and Sheriff Reese opened his eyes.

"River," he nodded to me. "Jordan."

One of the officers checked his watch and looked sternly to the Sheriff. "We don't have all night, Reese."

I looked to the officer who spoke. "We have evidence proving Mrs. Pots' innocence."

The officer cocked his brow and looked down at me with an amused look in his eye.

"Well, we have evidence suggesting an alternate suspect," Jordan said.

Sheriff Reese walked over to us. "What have you got?"

I paused and glanced around the room. "Can we go in the back?"

"Whatever you have, you should say it in front of everyone," Sheriff Reese said. "I'm no longer running this investigation."

"Who's in charge, then?" Jordan asked.

The officer standing before me turned to Jordan. "That would be me. Officer Trenton."

Jordan reached out to shake the man's hand. "O'Riley. I was with Boston until recently."

One of the other officers stepped forward and smiled. "Looking good there, O'Riley."

Jordan smiled. "Hey, Josh. Looking good, yourself."

The two men shook hands.

"Okay, enough with the friendly talk," I said. "We have evidence to suggest that Trey was murdered by his wife, Grace."

Sheriff Reese looked shocked. "Grace? Really? What proof do you have?"

"Motive," Jordan said. "We think she killed her husband to get take control of their restaurant business."

"Grace was on television," I added. "As the new owner of Trey's restaurant chain, she just announced their international expansion to a bunch of different countries around the world."

Officer Trenton crossed his arms. "And how exactly is this motive?"

"Trey wanted to close up shop," Jordan said. "He had planned to sell most of the restaurants and settle down here in Brimstone Bay."

"Only Grace had other plans," I said. "She didn't want to slow the business down, but didn't have much of a say in the plans for the restaurants while Trey was alive. She had no intention of settling down here."

"And where's this interview?" the Officer asked.

"It was just on TV," I said. "We watched it on the news less than half an hour ago."

"I'll go make some calls," Sheriff Reese said. He

went to the back room to try and track down a copy of the interview and left the rest of us together in the front office.

"Does this mean Mrs. Pots doesn't have to go to state prison?" I asked.

Trenton shook his head. "While the motive certainly seems plausible, I don't know if it's enough to let Nancy Pots off the hook. We have a first-hand witness as well as her confession that she gave the poisoned food item to the victim."

I rolled my eyes. "She didn't know it was poisoned. I don't understand how that's enough to put her in jail."

"Unintentional murder is still murder," he said. "It's called manslaughter."

"It's not unintentional murder," I snapped at him. "Mrs. Pots is a victim who was in the wrong place at the wrong time after Grace planted the poison cookie. Trey was murdered, and Mrs. Pots just got caught in the crossfire."

I sat down in one of the chairs along the back wall and placed my head in my hands. We had to find a way to convince everyone that Grace was the real suspect.

Well, first we had to confirm Grace was the killer, and then we would have to convince everyone about it.

Sheriff Reese came back into the room. "We've

got the interview on the computer. Everyone come into the board room, please."

We all crowded in to the back office around the Sheriff's laptop to watch the interview.

The interview began with a background story on Trey's restaurant business, and it lightly touched on Grace's restaurant as well. I hadn't realized her restaurant was doing so poorly.

The news feature made the merger out to be a romantic love story. Prince Charming swoops in with his successful restaurant business, then the damsel falls in love with him and he saves her business by merging both restaurants together. "A love story sweeter than pie," they were calling it. I felt sick to my stomach as I realized that it was likely the only reason Grace married Trey was to gain access to his successful dessert restaurant business.

I couldn't believe I considered that girl a friend.

"I don't see how any of this implicates Grace Wong," Officer Trenton finally said as the interview came to an end.

"You will once you hear the back story," I said.

Jordan moved to stand in front of the room and started telling the story from the beginning.

"Trey and I partnered up to open a small Desserti spin-off restaurant here in town after we found the old cafe for sale," he began. "We were old friends back in Boston, and I knew Trey since we were kids.

He had been getting overwhelmed by having so many restaurants, and he talked a lot about wanting to slow his business down quite a bit. He had plans to sell most of the restaurants, apart from the New York City one, and, of course, the new one we were starting together here in Brimstone Bay."

The room was quiet and everyone listened intently to Jordan as he spoke.

"Trey and Grace only met last year. They hit it off instantly and were engaged in only a few short months. They married in Vegas a few months ago, and Grace merged her restaurant with Trey's chain not long after." Jordan paused and rubbed his eyes. He looked like he was on the verge of tears, and I went to stand next to him and took his hand in mine. He smiled down at me before continuing his story.

"Trey was a really quiet guy, so I was surprised when they decided to marry in Vegas. It was out of character for him, but Grace really had a way of pulling him out of his shell. She was really good for his self-confidence."

Jordan pulled his hand from mine and began pacing the room.

"Trey wanted to settle down here. Start a family, and all that. As far as I understood, he even had buyers lined up for both the Seattle and Boston restaurants."

"Do you have any proof of this?" Jordan's officer friend Josh asked.

Jordan shrugged. "I'm sure there is. You could try contacting the restaurant managers, maybe."

"Were Mr. And Mrs. Wong co-owners of the restaurant chain?" Officer Trenton asked. "Do they have equal say in the business?"

"Again, I'm not sure."

"How about instead of interrogating Jordan, you bring Grace in for questioning? How's that for an idea?" I was growing impatient and was eager to get to the bottom of this. The sooner we got Grace's confession, the sooner Mrs. Pots could go home.

"Where is Mrs. Pots?" I asked.

"She's in the back room... secured," Sheriff Reese said. "Which reminds me, I should go check on her."

I raised my eyebrow at him as he walked towards the door. His emphasis on the word secured made me curious as to what he meant.

The Sheriff bent down toward me as he walked by and whispered in my ear. "She locked herself in the bathroom."

I suppressed a laugh and made it out to be a cough when I noticed all the officers in the room looking at me.

"So what are we going to do?" I asked. "Do you have enough to get Grace?"

Officer Trenton shook his head. "She hasn't done anything wrong. Unless she confesses, we don't have enough to justify accusing her of anything."

I gaped at him. "Okay, but surely you have enough to at least bring her in for questioning?"

He nodded. "Yes, we'll want to question Mrs. Wong."

"We'll have to be careful with that one," Jordan said. "She's clever. If she knows that we suspect her of murdering her husband, there's no way she will cooperate."

"I agree," I said. "We'll have to find a way to catch her in a lie. If you bring her in on suspicion of the crime, she'll find a way out of it. I know that girl."

"You keep saying 'we' as if you two have anything to do with this investigation," Officer Trenton said. "We appreciate you bringing the interview to our attention, but from here on out, I will be running this investigation. Understand?"

"Of course," Jordan said.

I sighed and very reluctantly agreed. "Sure, fine."

We would have to be clever with how we handled this and would have to come up with a plan to get Grace to admit she was the one responsible for the murder.

There was, of course, the chance that maybe we were wrong and Grace was simply taking advantage of the unfortunate situation with this whole expansion thing.

I pushed that thought from my mind for now.

Either way, we would have to bring her in and get her to talk.

"Why don't we get Jordan to invite her back to the shop to talk business?" I asked, the idea just popping into my head. I turned to Jordan who seemed intent on what I was saying.

"Offer to buy out her half of the restaurant," I continued. "We both know she has absolutely no interest in the Brimstone Bay location. I'm sure she'll be thrilled to come in and get rid of it. Use that as an excuse to get her to talk."

"Yeah, that could definitely work," Jordan said. "Only problem is, I don't have the finances to do that."

I shrugged. "She doesn't need to know that just yet. All we need to do is bring her in to talk."

"It's worth a shot," Officer Trenton said. "If that doesn't work, we can just call her in officially for questioning. She'll have to at least show up, or else she'll be breaking the law."

"Perfect," I said. "Could we set up a wire in the restaurant?" I looked up to Officer Trenton hopefully.

"Better yet, why don't you all just wait in the kitchen or the back room? I can lock the door and pretend there's electrical work being done in there or something," Jordan suggested.

"My work office is just upstairs from the restaurant," I added. "We could wait up there, as well, if we needed more space." There were five of the new officers, plus the Sheriff, myself, and I'm sure the Mayor wouldn't want to miss this either.

Officer Trenton nodded. "That will work well. We will tape everything, so we have it on record. But we should be close by in the event that she confesses to the crime."

Jordan brought out his phone and pulled Grace's number up.

"Put it on speaker so we can hear," I suggested.

We all quieted as his phone began to ring.

"Jordan!" Grace's voice boomed through the speaker phone. "Just the man I wanted to talk to."

"Hey, Grace, how are you doing?" Jordan asked.

"Oh, you know, keeping myself distracted. It's the only thing I really can do to keep myself from breaking down."

"I understand completely," Jordan feigned sympathy. "Hey, look, I want to talk to you about the restaurant."

"Oh, perfect. I've been wanting to talk to you about the same. Are you free to meet in half an hour?"

Jordan looked to me with a confused expression, and I shrugged my shoulders.

"Are you in town?" he asked.

"Sure am. Just got up here from New York. Been hiding away at my sister's place the past few days to get away from everything."

I rolled my eyes. Well, that was at least one lie we had caught her in.

"Half an hour sounds good," Jordan answered. "See you at the restaurant in thirty."

Jordan hung up the phone and turned to me. "So, it seems she's no longer in Italy."

"Guess the interview was pre-recorded," I said. "Must have filmed yesterday or something. I know for a fact that she wasn't at her sister's last night."

I explained to the officers that the girls and I had driven down to New York City yesterday and stayed with Grace's sister, Emily, who had told us that Grace was away at a counselling camp.

Officer Trenton nodded thoughtfully. "Well, that doesn't bode well for Grace."

He then turned to his other officers and instructed them to head out to the restaurant to set up the recording device. "We'll need you there, too," he said to Jordan.

Jordan nodded. "Sure. I'll meet you guys there in a minute."

"I'll come, too," I said. "I should probably go check the office to make sure JoAnn's not still there feeling sorry for herself."

Sheriff Reese reached out and grabbed my shoulder as I turned to follow Jordan out the door.

"What were you doing in New York?" I couldn't read his expression, but I treaded carefully.

I sighed. "We traced the spell that killed Trey to a place in the city."

Sheriff Reese stared incredulously at me. "And you didn't mention this before, why?"

"Other things came up," I said. He crossed his arms and gave me as stern a look.

"Did you find the source?" he asked.

I nodded. "We found the guy who sold the spell. Said the person who bought it was a woman, and talked a lot about baking."

Sheriff Reese's mouth hung open. "River, that's absolutely something you needed to come to me with. That is crucial information."

I shrugged. "Well, you're not in charge of the investigation anymore, so what does it matter?"

The Sheriff looked as if his head was going to explode. "Do you know what this means? That suggests Mrs. Pots was the one to buy the spell."

"Or Grace," I said. "It won't matter once we get a confession from Grace, anyway."

Sheriff Reese inhaled a deep breath and slowly exhaled, steadying himself. "Is there anything else you failed to mention?"

I thought for a moment, then decided there was no sense hiding anything further from him.

"Yeah, Zack Brendon visited the building before we arrived."

"The journalist at the Brimstone Press?" he asked.

I nodded. "Yeah, he threatened the guy inside before we got there. Said he'd kill him if he talked. I don't really know what that was about."

"Is Zack involved in some way?"

"My guess is he found out we were going down there and wanted to beat us to it. Anything for a story, you know?"

The sheriff nodded slowly. "That guy does give me a bad taste in my mouth. This is certainly worth looking into more, though."

I smiled. "Absolutely. I'd initiate a full investigation into him if I were you. You never know what other motives he may have had for visiting the dealer."

I was ninety-nine percent sure that Zack was just being Zack, and wanted desperately to get the full story before I did. But the thought of him being under investigation made me quite happy.

"Do you know the name of the guy who sold the spell? That's a criminal offense, River. He should be in jail, especially given the outcome."

I shook my head. "He made us promise to leave the cops out of it before he gave us any information. Besides, he got the spell from a friend of his. He was just the middle man, or so he says."

Sheriff Reese nodded. "Alright, but I would like to look into this further. If you give me his name, I won't arrest him unless we find anything else against him. I do want to look more into where he got that spell, though. Magic like that is insanely illegal, and selling that stuff could land you a lifetime in jail."

"Sure. Steve Jameson. Runs a laundromat in Chinatown."

"Thanks, River."

Jordan honked the car from outside, and I waved backward to Sheriff Reese as I ran out the door.

"See you there," I called back to him.

CHAPTER FIFTEEN

JORDAN LET THE OFFICERS INTO THE RESTAURANT through the back door to avoid any attention on the street. Less than two minutes later, Sheriff Reese arrived with Mayor Scott. It was a full house, to say the least.

The officers got busy installing the recording device in the restaurant downstairs, and I went up to the office to see if JoAnn was still there.

Unfortunately for her, she was, and she was balling her eyes out something fierce.

"What happened?" I asked as I ran over to her. I kneeled in front of her and took her by the hands.

JoAnn sniffed and took a steadying breath. "It's Zack."

I sighed. "What about Zack?"

I pretty much knew the answer before she said it. His chauvinistic attitude, the way he treats women, the way he talks down to everyone who he thinks is below him… take your pick.

"He's sleeping with Grace."

I blinked. Well, that's a new one.

"What are you talking about?" I asked. I pulled my hands back and stood up. "Zack and Grace Wong?"

JoAnn nodded and wiped the tears from her eyes. "I saw them through the restaurant window as I was walking by this morning. They were definitely not being discreet about it. I'm not sure they realized some of the newspapers covering the front window had peeled away. Apart from a large suitcase on the floor in front of them hiding their legs, they were going at it for all to see."

I couldn't believe my ears. "And you're sure you saw… what you think you saw?"

JoAnn crossed her arms, and her eyebrows went up. "Yes, River, I know what I saw. Hard to mistake what two naked bodies on the floor are doing."

I squeezed my eyes shut and tried to rid my head of the visuals. "Thanks for that, now that's all I can see."

"How do you think I feel?" JoAnn asked. She stood up and began pacing the room. "I can't believe him."

"Did they see you?"

"They saw me, all right." A mischievous grin grew on JoAnn's face. "They nearly jumped ten feet in the air when I began banging my fists against the window."

My eyes went wide. "How did they react?"

"Grace didn't seem fazed," JoAnn said. "But Zack looked embarrassed. Came up to the office barely clothed to try and explain."

"What did you say?"

She shrugged. "I told him his services were no longer required. By me, or by the Brimstone Press."

I smiled and was cheering loudly in my head. "Way to go, JoAnn. Serves him right for being such a hurtful ass."

"Yeah." JoAnn's eyes filled with tears again as she sat down at her desk and looked up at me. "I'm sorry you had to witness this."

I shook my head. "Don't be sorry. Zack's the one that should be sorry. I can't believe he was having an affair with Grace…"

I paused, then gasped as I began piecing everything together. "That's why Zack was in New York."

"I'm sorry?"

"Never mind. JoAnn, I have to go. If you see the slimy bastard, could you tell him I'm looking for him?"

She nodded and smiled through her tears. "He really is a slimy bastard."

"Always was, always will be," I said. "I hope

you feel better. Sorry, you have to go through all of this."

I waved goodbye to JoAnn and raced down the stairs to the restaurant. I thought I probably shouldn't use the front door in case Grace was nearby, so I ran around the back of the building and joined everyone in the back room slash kitchen area of what once was the cafe.

"Zack's involved," I said through heavy breathing.

"What now?" Officer Trenton turned to look at me with a heavy expression on his face. "Who's involved?"

I rested my back against the wall and tried to regain my breath. I was so out of shape; I really needed to get back into running.

"What did he do?" Jordan was staring at me, eagerly waiting for me to continue.

"I'll give you the Sparknotes version," I said to Officer Trenton. "Zack Brendon is a journalist who I work with at the paper. Yesterday morning, my housemates and I drove down to New York City to check the address we traced the spell to that killed Trey."

"Spell? What spell?" Officer Trenton did not look impressed.

I ignored him and continued. "When we arrived, we saw Zack there. I thought initially he was just there for a story, as he apparently had asked the owner of the place a bunch of questions about the murder. He was also concerned about whether other people had come to question him or not."

I paused to catch my breath, wiping a bead of sweat from my brow. Honestly, I only ran about twenty feet. I was going to get back into running first thing tomorrow morning.

"Turns out, Zack is in a relationship with Grace Wong," I continued. "He was likely down there trying to cover up her tracks; to make sure no one finds out that she was the one who bought the dark magic spell that killed her husband."

The room was so quiet you could hear a pin drop.

Finally, Jordan spoke. "Grace was having an affair with Zack?"

I nodded. "JoAnn just told me. She saw them together earlier today."

"I don't believe it," he said. "She and Trey were happy."

I rolled my eyes. "Jordan, haven't we already come to the conclusion that Grace married Trey for his restaurant business? Trey may have been happy, but I doubt Grace was."

Jordan shook his head. "Trey deserved better."

"He did."

"Alright, back to the matter at hand," Office Trenton said. "Jordan, I trust you haven't forgotten your training from when you were in the force? Let's see what we can get out of Mrs. Wong, okay?"

Jordan straightened his jacket nervously and turned to leave through the kitchen door. I heard the door lock and his footsteps on the other side as he paced.

It had nearly been half an hour, and we expected Grace's arrival anytime. Everyone in the back room held their silence, and I could feel nervous energy building all around me.

I sat down against the wall and listened.

Not two minutes later, Grace arrived. Her voice was exuberant, and we could hear her clearly through the back wall.

"So happy you called," she said. "I've been thinking about this place all day."

"Me, too," I heard Jordan say.

"I know Trey was keen on running this place with you," Grace began, "but I really need to focus on his dreams of expanding his restaurant empire. I'm sure Trey told you how important it was for him that the restaurant chain grew."

I held my breath as I listened through the long silence that followed Grace's question.

"Failed to mention it." Jordan spoke through gritted teeth, and I could tell he was livid.

"Well, that's all he wanted, so, I'm going to make it my life mission to grant his wish," she said.

"But that will involve getting rid of this place, so I can focus on the bigger picture."

"You would know best," Jordan said.

"I appreciate the confidence. It's just that, with Trey gone, I really need to step up my game and do my best to fill his shoes. I need to focus, and, in order to do so, I need to get rid of Brimstone Bay. It just reminds me so much of him, you know?"

"I'll buy out Trey's half of the business," Jordan said.

"Oh, splendid." Grace sounded beyond pleased. "You can have it for a bargain. I just want to get rid of it. There's just too many bad memories associated with this place, after what happened."

"Speaking about what happened," Jordan began. I sat up and pressed my ear against the wall to be sure I didn't miss anything. "The cops think they can trace the spell back to the original owner."

Grace paused for a moment. "Oh yeah? Well, that's really great, isn't it?" Her voice wasn't as perky as it had been before. "Do they have any leads?"

Her voice raised an octave, and maybe it was just me, but I thought her voice sounded a bit panicky.

"What have you heard?" Grace asked.

I imagined Jordan was trying to come up with some sort of plan, as there was a long moment of silence before he finally spoke.

"Well, don't tell anyone this, as they don't

know for certain, but I think it might be Zack Brandon." Jordan paused, and when Grace didn't say anything he continued. "You probably don't know him. He works at the Brimstone Press with River."

My eyes went wide, and I looked up to Officer Trenton. He shrugged and looked just as confused as I was. What was Jordan playing at? I hoped he had a plan.

"Oh, well, no. Not really," Grace finally answered. "Any idea why they suspect him?"

"Something about New York. I'm not sure, really."

"I see."

I stood up and joined Officer Trenton near the door. "We've got to get Zack in there," I whispered. "She'll be more likely to talk to Zack than to Jordan, I think."

The officer nodded, and I whipped out my phone immediately.

Have a lead for a story, I texted Zack. *Meet at the restaurant for a chat?*

My phone buzzed back immediately. *Sure. See you in ten,* the message said.

"He's on his way," I whispered to the officer.

Officer Trenton nodded and looked down at me. "Get Jordan out of there. I'd like to get Mrs. Wong and Mr. Miller together alone."

"Sure thing," I whispered back.

I send Jordan a text telling him to leave ASAP. I hope Grace couldn't see his phone.

I heard Jordan's phone beep from the other room.

"Why don't I go get the contract that Trey and I signed for the restaurant? Might as well get this all sorted tonight. The papers are in my apartment, though. Mind hanging out for twenty minutes while I go get them?"

"Sure, doll," Grace said. "I'll be here."

I heard the front door close, and a minute later Jordan joined us in the back of the building.

"What's going on?" he asked.

"Zack's on his way," I said. "Thought he and Grace might want to have a chat."

Jordan's eyebrows shot up. "Nice one."

The front door chimed open, and we all fell silent again to listen.

"What are you doing here?" Grace sounded surprised.

"Meeting River about a work thing."

"Here, in the restaurant?"

"I'm assuming she spoke with JoAnn," he answered. "Pretty sure I'm not welcome in the office anymore."

"Fair enough," Grace said. "This would all have been a lot easier if that damned woman hadn't been spying on us."

There was a long silence, or a break from talking

at least, as kissing noises emanated through the walls.

I faked a gag and looked up to Jordan. "We're not getting anywhere," I whispered.

I brought out my phone again and began typing out a message.

"What are you doing?" Officer Trenton whispered to me.

"Stirring the pot," I answered.

He looked angry but didn't stop me.

Running a bit late, I texted Zack. *Is it true the cops saw you in New York talking to the guy who sold the spell that killed Trey?*

I put my phone back in my pocket and waited.

"What did you do?" Officer Trenton growled at me.

I smiled. "Just wait."

The kissing noises stopped and were replaced by Zack's loud swearing. "Oh, Shit!"

"What? What happened?"

A loud bang came from the front room, and I assumed Zack had pounded his fists against the wall or a table or something.

"They saw me talking to Steve," Zack said loudly.

"Who did? What are you talking about?"

"The cops! They saw me with Steve. They know he was the one who sold the spell."

"You're kidding?" Grace sounded worried. "How do you know?"

I rolled my eyes. Jordan had just told Grace the cops suspected Zack, but she obviously wasn't concerned with telling him what she knew.

"River is buddy-buddy with the damn cops in town," he answered. "She must have heard something. Dammit!"

I heard another loud bang and then a serious of particularly creative swear words.

"I'm not being thrown in jail for *your* God damn crime, Grace!" Zack was shouting now, and sounded absolutely furious.

"Shut up," Grace snapped. I heard the front door's lock click. "Someone might hear you."

"I don't care if they freaking hear me," Zack shouted. "I went down to make sure that pesky witch and her damned friends didn't talk to the guy, and now they think I'm the one responsible for all of this."

"Calm down, Zack," Grace said. "You don't know that."

"Get your damn hands off of me," Zack shouted. A louder bang sounded, and from Grace's muffled cry I imagined he had thrown her against the wall.

"You've done nothing wrong," Grace said slowly. "For all they know, you were just buying a joint or something. It's not a big deal."

"Not a big deal?" Zack was shouting again.

"NOT A BIG DEAL? You buy a spell to kill your fucking husband, and I'm the one they see at the source! You're telling me that's not a big deal?"

"We'll figure this out, babe," Grace said. "Just calm down. We'll figure it out together."

"Don't babe me, you cheating whore."

"Don't! Call! Me! A! Whore!" Grace was shouting now, and she sounded beyond livid.

Loud crashes began sounding from the front room, followed by a series of shouts and swearing. It sounded like a full-on brawl was taking place on the other side of the door.

"Do we have enough to get her yet?" I whispered to Officer Trenton, who had one hand on the doorknob, ready to interfere if things got out of hand.

By the noises coming from the other room, it seemed to me that they had already reached that point.

He shook his head. "We need to hear it from her."

"I'm not going to jail for you," Zack shouted through the crashes and bangs. "I'll tell them the truth if they bring me in."

"Good luck with that," Grace sneered. "You have no proof that I did it. The sleazy dealer didn't even see my face when I picked up the goods. You have no way of proving that I did it."

"I'll find a way," Zack snapped back.

An even louder crash sounded, and Grace screamed. I jumped up and nearly pushed Officer Trenton out of the way to go stop the fight, but he held his hand out to stop me.

We all stood tense, waiting for the right opportunity to interfere with whatever was going on in the restaurant on the other side of the wall.

Grace screamed again, and the deafening bang of a gun shot went off. Everyone in the back room threw themselves on the ground.

"Was that a gun?" I whispered. "Did one of them shoot a damn gun?" My heart was racing, and my voice sounded frantic.

I waited, wide-eyed and cold from shock until finally, we heard both their voices speak from the other room.

"You could have shot me, you crazy bitch!" Zack shouted.

"Well, it got your attention, didn't it?" Grace snapped. "Shut up and listen to me."

I hear a soft thud from the other room as if Zack has dropped some sort of weapon he may have been holding. Likely a piece of wood or a tool from the renovation.

"So what if they saw you? That doesn't prove anything. The only thing that matters is that pathetic husband of mine is dead, and I finally have complete control over the business. That stupid fool was going to let all of our hard work die by selling off most of our restaurants."

"His hard work, you mean," Zack snapped. "His restaurants."

Grace must have slapped him, as I recognized the painful sound of flesh on flesh before Zack swore loudly.

"My hard work, now. The restaurants are mine. I'm going to build an empire, and if you're smart, you'll come with me out of this damned garbage pit of a town and move back to New York where I can run the businesses."

"And if they trace the spell back to you?" Zack asked.

"Impossible," Grace answered. "They'll find no traces of it anywhere. I put the whole damned thing into the cookie. The only person who saw me do it was Trey, and he was too pathetically trusting and love-sick that he didn't even clue in to what I was doing."

Zack began laughing as Grace recounted the events.

"All I had to do was pretend to like that damn woman's disgusting baking, and when I put the cookie back down on the table, she offered it to Trey. It was too damned easy to get rid of that pathetic excuse for a man."

I looked up pleading into Officer Trenton's eyes, who finally nodded and unlocked the back door.

"Stay here, and don't move," he said to us. "She's got a gun, and I wouldn't put it past her to use it again."

I reluctantly nodded and looked around to everyone else who nodded as well.

Officer Trenton then brought out his own gun and stormed into the restaurant.

CHAPTER SIXTEEN

"PUT YOUR HANDS WHERE I CAN SEE THEM," Officer Trenton shouted from the other room.

Through Zack's swearing, I could barely hear Grace speak. "B..b..but Officer, I don't know what you mean. What's happening?"

"There was a gunshot not minutes ago," Trenton said. "I see the gun on the table. Put your hands up where I can see them, and step away from the table."

"Officer, please, I didn't do anything," Zack mumbled. It sounded like he was crying.

Good, that man needed to be put in his place.

"Mrs. Wong, you're under arrest for the murder of Trey Wong."

"What are you talking about?" Grace asked. "This is absurd. I had nothing to do with my poor husband's murder. How dare you accuse a grieving widow of such a heinous crime."

"We can do this the easy way, or we can do this the hard way. You choose, Mrs. Wong."

"Put those handcuffs away, you bully," Grace said.

"As I said, Mrs. Wong. The easy way or the hard way."

"Fine. But I have weak elbows; you'll have to cuff my wrists in the front."

After a lot of swearing and crying, I heard the click of handcuffs.

I took this as my cue that it was safe in there, and stepped through the door into the room. Jordan, Sheriff Reese, and the rest of the gang followed close behind.

"River?" Grace stared at me with wide eyes. "What are you doing here? What's happening?"

"We've got you, Grace," I answered. "I should have suspected you from the start. I don't know how I was so blind. Your marriage to such a kind, sweet guy should have been my first clue. You'd never settle for someone quiet like that in a million years if it didn't mean you got something out of it."

Grace rolled her eyes. "Oh, please, you wouldn't have suspected me if I had shot him directly in front of your eyes."

"What's that supposed to mean?" I glared daggers at the girl. I was finding it harder and harder to believe I actually liked her once.

"It means," Grace spat, "that your life is all

sunshine and freaking rainbows, and since moving to this pathetic little town, you've lost all grasp of the real world."

One of the other officers took the gun from the table, and the others joined Officer Trenton in surrounding Grace and Zack.

I rolled my eyes. "You know, Grace, given your current position, I would suggest sucking up to me rather than insulting me."

She brushed her long bangs off her face with her handcuffed hands. I had to hand it to Grace; she still managed to look cool, despite being all disheveled, handcuffed, and accused of murder.

"I'm not in any position," Grace said. "You've got nothing on me. You won't be able to prove anything, and I'll be let go before we even reach the damn prison."

I thought to myself for a moment and then smirked.

"So you think."

My expression seemed to throw her off. "What do you mean?" Her confidence was wavering, and I was enjoying watching her squirm.

"Meaning," I began. I cleared my voice for dramatic effect. "That I was the one to speak to your little New York friend, Steve."

Both Grace and Zack's eyes went wide, and I smiled back at them.

"And let's just say," I continued, "that he had interesting things to say."

"Liar!" Grace shouted at me. "That greasy little rat never even saw me."

I rolled my eyes, then laughed out loud when she realized that she just implicated herself again with that last statement. "Man, you're making this way too easy, Gracie."

I turned to Zack. "And you, you disrespectful little worm. I saw you leave the laundromat the morning we went to check it out. Poor Steve seemed a bit shaken up after your visit. I thought, at first, that you just wanted to beat me to the story, but it's clear now that you were just trying to cover up your new girlfriend's trail."

Zack began shaking his head frantically, his eyes wild and terrified. "I didn't know," he said. "I promise, I had no idea. I went because she asked me to. Honest. I didn't know." He was crying into his hands on the ground at this point, his body convulsing from his sobbing.

"Pathetic," Grace spat at him. "I'm embarrassed for you right now, Zack. You're just as whiney as my husband."

After a few minutes of his desperate pleading and complete breakdown on the floor, I started to feel sorry for the guy. He was an absolute ass, and he deserved to be punished for what he did to JoAnn and Trey, but it was possible that he didn't actually have anything to do with this. Given Grace's other numerous deceptions, I wouldn't put it past her to have simply used him as a pawn in her evil scheme.

"Grace, I don't think you understand the gravity of what you've done," I told her. She seemed so calm and relaxed. "You murdered your husband, and we heard you admit it. You're going to jail."

"For a very, very long time," Jordan said. He had stayed relatively quiet throughout this whole thing. I made the mistake of looking back at him, and my heart nearly shattered. His eyes were red and puffy, and his face was whiter than a ghost.

And yes, I know, ghosts aren't actually white. It's just an expression. So, sue me.

"We've got you on tape admitting to murder, Mrs. Wong," Officer Trenton said. He was standing beside her, his hand firmly grasping her shoulder.

Grace blinked, and her expression began to change as the reality of what was happening seemed to finally come crashing down on her. She began to shake.

"No, it was a mistake," she said frantically. "It wasn't me. I was just talking big."

"You did something terrible, Grace," I said. "You're not getting out of this one."

Grace's eyes grew wild. "It was him!" she shouted as she pointed towards Zack on the ground. "You saw him with your own eyes. He went back to cover his tracks. He did it so he could be with me!"

"Don't implicate me in your mess," Zack shouted back. "You're an evil, power-hungry whore with no conscience."

"You said you loved me," Grace yelled. She was crying now. "You told me you loved me, remember?"

"How could I love such a monster?" Zack pushed himself up and tried to steady his breathing with a few deep breaths.

"I did it for you," Grace sobbed. "Baby, you can't let me go to jail. Do something. Save me."

"You didn't do this for me," Zack spat. "You did this to advance your career."

Grace screamed a loud, blood-curdling scream, and everyone in the room covered their ears to protect themselves from the nearly inhuman sound.

She then took advantage the opportunity and twisted out of Officer Trenton's grip, and lunged forward toward the officer with the gun.

"Grace, no!" I called.

But it was too late. Grace ripped the gun from the unsuspecting officer's hand and waved it above her head as best she could with both hands cuffed together, and she continued screaming at the top of her lungs.

She shot two shots into the ceiling before Officer Trenton threw himself at her and tackled her onto the floor.

On her way down, she fired a third shot at the

room, and a number of us screamed and threw ourselves onto the ground. My body shook as I pressed my face to the floor, my hands covering my head instinctively.

I never understood why characters in movies reacted that way to a gun shot. It's not like your hands covering your head could stop a bullet. I began to laugh nervously to myself at the thought. Who knew I would ever experience it first-hand? At least, now, I understood the reaction.

The officers in the room sprung to action immediately, but I felt like the world was moving in slow motion around me. My ears were ringing, and I watched as Grace was dragged out of the room and the gun was seized by another officer.

I slowly pushed myself up off the ground. My heart was pounding, and Jordan wrapped his arms around me and held me close as I shook.

A moment later, he pushed away from me and stepped towards Zack, who didn't seem to be moving.

"Zack?" I asked, kneeling down beside him after following Jordan's lead. When he didn't answer, I put my hand on his shoulder and pushed him over so he would look at me.

Zack's lifeless form fell backward toward to floor, revealing a gunshot wound in the middle of his chest.

"Oh, my God," I jumped back and stared down at him. "Oh, my God!" I screamed.

Jordan threw himself down on the ground next to Zack and listened for his breathing. He then felt for a pulse on both his neck and his wrist, and immediately placed his hands on his chest to begin CPR.

I watched as he withdrew his hand after the first compression, his hands dripping with blood from the wound.

Jordan looked up at me and shook his head. "He's dead."

I fell to my knees and stared at the body. "I.." I couldn't formulate a coherence sentence. I took a shallow, shuttering breath and tried again to speak. "But he was just alive."

Jordan wiped the blood from his hands onto his pants and came to wrap his arms around me again. I couldn't stop shaking, and could barely hear Jordan's words of comfort that he was whispering into my ear.

The officer Jordan called Josh came back into the room, and took in the scene.

"Dammit," he swore. He moved towards the body and went through the same motions that Jordan had done.

"He's dead," I said, stating the obvious.

"Yes," Josh agreed.

Josh looked up to Jordan with a sympathetic

look on his face. "Why don't you take her home. We'll call you for a statement later. Right now, we've got our hands full."

Jordan nodded. "Alright. Thank you."

Sheriff Reese was in the back, helping the other officers deal with Grace. We passed Mayor Scott on our way out of the restaurant. The Mayor looked solemn and didn't speak. He was simply looking down at the body and shaking his head.

Jordan put his hand on the Mayor's shoulder, who then snapped his head up as if he was breaking himself from a trance.

"Why don't you go home," Jordan said. "Sheriff Reese and the officers can handle this. Go home and relax. We can grab a beer tomorrow and talk about this if you like."

The Mayor nodded and Jordan patted him on the back and he walked by us and out of the restaurant without saying a word. I sometimes forgot they were friends, but, right then, I was grateful for it. Mayor Scott would have a mess to deal with once word got out about what happened, and I was glad that he had someone to talk to about it to keep him sane.

"My sweater," I said as Jordan pulled me through the front door of the restaurant.

He raised his eyebrow and looked down at me. "What about your sweater?"

"Office," I said. I was finding complete sentences difficult. I suspected that I was in shock.

Jordan nodded then led me towards the office door. It was unlocked, and we headed upstairs to my work to get my sweater.

I stopped abruptly when we reached the upstairs door and stared into the room at the scene that lay before us.

JoAnn was cowering in the back corner; her hands were over her ears, and she was rocking back and forth. Her face was pale and she didn't even seem to notice we had come in.

There were three bullet holes in the floor around her desk.

"Oh, my God," I said. I ran over to JoAnn and held her face in my hands.

"JoAnn," I spoke gently to her, and she slowly met my gaze. "JoAnn, are you okay?"

"The floor has holes in it," she said after a long moment.

"It does. Grace had a gun."

JoAnn stared at me with wide eyes then nodded.

I glanced back to Jordan who was already on the phone.

Jordan muttered a few words and hung up, and not a minute later Mayor Scott walked through the door.

He walked over to JoAnn and crouched down next to me.

"Hey, JoAnn," he said. "Why don't we get you

out of here? Let's go back to my office and have some hot tea, okay?"

JoAnn looked up to him and nodded. "Yeah, sure. Thanks. That would be nice."

He helped her up, and I handed her the jacket that was on the back of her chair.

"Thank you," she managed a half smile.

"You okay?" I repeated. I really didn't know what else to say.

She shrugged. "Yeah, I think so. Sorry. Just a bit… shaken up. There are holes in the floor."

I hugged her and could feel she was still shaking. The two of us felt like cold Chihuahuas, unable to stop our shivering.

"I'll have this repaired as soon as I can," Jordan said, motioning to the floors.

JoAnn nodded. "Was anyone hurt?"

I exchanged looks with Mayor Scott and Jordan.

"Why don't we go have that tea," Mayor Scott said.

I smiled at JoAnn. "That sounds like a great idea. We'll chat soon."

The Mayor led JoAnn out of the office, leaving Jordan and me alone.

I reached my hands for him, and he pulled me in for another hug. I pressed my face into his chest and tried to force myself to not think about what had just happened downstairs. He smelt like vanilla and sawdust, and I focused on his scent, allowing it to consume my thoughts. I felt calmed, and, after a few minutes, I could have easily fallen asleep in his arms.

"Why don't we go to your place," Jordan said. "Let's get away from here."

"That sounds great."

Jordan held my hand and led me down the stairs and to his car that was parked just down the street. He helped me into the passenger seat and buckled my seatbelt for me. It was as if I had lost all ability to function properly, and all I could do was stare forward and try to maintain even breathing.

"It's normal to experience shock after witnessing something like that," he said soothingly to me. He squeezed my hand after climbing into the driver's seat and started the car.

I looked out the window and nodded. "Okay."

"Let's get you home," he said.

We took off down the street, the flashing lights of the police cars fading behind us as we drove away together in silence.

CHAPTER SEVENTEEN

BAILEY, RORY, AND JANE WERE WAITING FOR ME AT the house when we arrived, and I could tell by their expressions that they were not expecting to see me looking the way I did.

Jordan walked me into the house, and the girls stepped aside to let us through.

It was a testament to how great my housemates were that they recognized how distraught I was and didn't bombard me with questions the moment I came home.

"I'll make tea," Rory said right away, rushing down the stairs to Mrs. Brody's apartment.

Mrs. Brody appeared a moment later and looked me up and down. "Better come down, dear."

Jordan looked down at me, and I nodded my approval. We walked down the stairs to the basement apartment, hand in hand, and I curled up in a ball on the old vintage couch in the living room.

Jane and Bailey sat beside me on the couch, and Jordan found a seat on the chair opposite me.

"Here's some tea. It's a blend of chamomile and citrus." Rory brought a tray with a tea pot and six cups on it a few minutes later.

"Let me help with that," Mrs. Brody said. She ran back into the kitchen and rummaged through her large cabinet and brought out a jar filled with some sort of dark crushed herbs.

"This will make you feel better." She brought the jar over to us and sprinkled the herbs into my tea cup.

"Looks like you could do with some, too, dear," she said to Jordan. She sprinkled the herbs into his cup as well before he had a chance to protest.

We all sipped the tea in silence, and I could feel everyone's eyes on me.

Whatever Mrs. Brody put in the tea, I was grateful for it. I could feel the warmth filling my body; a sense of calm washing over me.

A soft meowing came from the far side of the room, and three adorable little cats came walking towards us. Big fat Momma and her little kitten Agnes flopped down on the floor at Mrs. Brody's feet, and Soot came and jumped up on my lap.

As per usual, he flopped on his back, expecting

tummy rubs and attention. Leave it to the cat to make everything about him.

"So," Bailey said after a few moments of silence. She glanced nervously between Jordan and me. "Was the date that bad?"

I nearly spit out my tea as I laughed. I supposed that's how everything must have looked to them. The last we spoke, I was headed out on my date with Jordan.

"Wasn't the best date in the world, I'll admit that much," Jordan said.

I did my best to smile. "Yeah, it could have gone better."

Everyone seemed even more confused by what we had said, and my housemates sat there staring at me as I sipped my tea.

I sighed and rubbed my eyes, trying to think of the best way to summarize the events of the past few hours.

"Grace Wong is in jail, and Zack Brendon is dead."

Silence. I sipped my tea as I let my words sink in with those around me.

"Grace is in jail," Rory repeated.

"Yes," I said.

"Zack is dead," Bailey repeated.

"Yes."

"What the heck did you guys do on your date?" Jane asked.

While it may not have been appropriate given the situation, I couldn't help but laugh. I let the laughter consume me, and soon the whole room was laughing. It felt good, and I could sense the tension leave my body.

I wiped tears from my eyes and tried to bring myself back to the present moment.

"Tell us what happened, dear," Mrs. Brody said.

I blew out a sigh and prepared myself to relive the events of the evening.

"Jordan and I saw an interview with Grace on TV during our date. She was all excited about expanding Trey's restaurant chain and just announced their opening in Italy," I said.

"We clued in right away," Jordan continued. "Trey never would have allowed the expansion if he were alive. He wanted to settle down and sell off some of his restaurants, but Grace was lying on TV, saying that it was Trey's dream to expand."

"So, you're saying Grace is the murderer?" Bailey asked. Everyone in the room looked shocked.

I nodded. "Yeah, and we got her to confess on tape."

"Wow," Rory said. "I can't believe that."

"She seemed genuinely upset at the party," Bailey said. "I didn't think there was any way someone could fake that sort of emotion."

I shrugged. "She's a good actress, I guess."

"And what did you mean about Zack? How can he be dead?" Jane asked.

"Grace shot him," I said, rubbing my temples in attempt to subside the headache that I could feel building in the back of my head.

"What?" Rory stared at me incredulously. "I don't understand."

"Turns out he was covering up her tracks," I said. "When we saw him in New York, he wasn't there to steal the story. He was there trying to protect Grace."

"And she shot him because of it?" Rory asked.

I shook my head. "After we caught her in her lie, the police stormed in and arrested her. Only, she had a gun and ended up shooting at the room. Jordan and I were lucky we didn't get shot. Zack wasn't so lucky."

Mrs. Brody was shaking her head as if she wouldn't believe what she was hearing. "Those poor boys."

"Wait, so this means Mrs. Pots is clear?" Rory asked.

I blinked and sat up. "Oh, yeah, I completely forgot. She must be out by now."

Mrs. Brody pushed herself up from her chair. "I'd better go check on her. Make sure she's okay."

"I'll come, too," Jane said.

"Same," Bailey added.

"I want to come, too" Rory agreed. "River, are you coming?"

I shook my head. "No, thanks. I don't think I can handle that right now. I just need some space."

Rory came over and put her hand on my shoulder. "Is there anything you need?"

"No, thanks," I smiled. "I'll be fine. I just need to sleep, I think. Give Mrs. Pots a big hug for me, will you?"

Rory nodded. "She'll be wanting to give you one in person, I'd imagine, seeing as you're the one responsible for setting her free."

"And Jordan," I said. "He was pretty much the brains behind the operation."

Jordan smiled and I winked back at him.

I then began to blush because I realized how stupid I must have looked winking at him like an idiot.

I hid my head in my hands and willed myself to magically disappear. Unfortunately, my magic doesn't work that way.

Mrs. Brody and the girls left to go to the Sheriff's office to see Mrs. Pots, leaving Jordan and me alone in the house.

"I need some fresh air," I said.

Jordan nodded. "Sure. Where?"

"Let's go down to the beach," I suggested. The waves were calming, and I was beginning to become a firm believer that the salty sea air could cure just about anything.

Jordan and I walked through the yard, which still had the decorations up from the party, and descended the steep staircase down the bluffs to the beach below.

The night was windy, and the waves crashed hard against the shore. The immense noise from the ocean made my problems seem small, and it was a refreshing feeling.

Jordan held my hand as we walked.

"So, does this mean we're dating now?" he asked.

I laughed. "I don't know. Does it?"

"Well, we went on a date," he said. "And I did make you weak in the knees that one time."

I nudged him with my shoulder as we walked. "Did not."

"Did, too," he said. "Besides, I plan on taking you out on more dates, so I think that technically means we're dating."

"Technically," I agreed.

The moment was ruined when my phone rang, and I saw Sheriff Reese's number appear on my screen.

"Better answer that," Jordan said. "Could be important."

I sighed and swiped my phone to answer.

"Hey, Sheriff," I said.

"We found the original source of the spell," the sheriff said.

I stopped walked and turned to Jordan.

"How? Who was it?" I asked.

Jordan raised his eyebrows, but didn't interrupt.

"That Steve guy was quite the talker, apparently. They took him in for questioning in New York, and got the name of the man who gave him the spell that killed Trey Wong. He was arrested about an hour ago."

"Who was it?" I asked.

"Some bartender from one of those underground nightclubs," he said. "Apparently, he's a shifter, or whatever you call those people these days. Miles Cochrane."

I froze in place. "Miles from Shine nightclub?"

"That's the one. You know him?"

"No, but I know someone who does. Thanks, Sheriff."

I hung up the phone and stared wide-eyed at Jordan. My headache began to come back full force, and my head felt like it was about to explode.

"What's going on?" Jordan asked.

"They arrested the man responsible for the spell."

Jordan smiled. "Well, that's good, isn't it? Why do you look so stressed?"

I let out a loud sigh and continued walking,

pulling Jordan behind me as I pressed forward through the heavy wind.

"Let's just say Bailey has really bad taste in men."

Jordan seemed to understand and didn't press the issue further.

I had no idea how I was going to break the news to Bailey. First, she falls for a local guy who turns out to be a murderer. Then, she falls for a criminal who sells dark magic spells that kill people. There's not enough ice cream in the world to soothe that girl's soon-to-be re-broken heart.

We walked farther down the rocky beach, and I let the rhythmic sound of the crashing waves wash away all the stressful thoughts in my mind.

There was a long rocky outcrop that projected far out into the bay toward one of the lighthouses, and Jordan took my hand and led me over the rocks away from the beach.

When we reached the edge, we stood there and looked out over the ocean. It felt like a different world out here, completely separated from all the trouble and stresses of the mainland.

"So, tell me about these dates you plan on taking me on," I said.

Jordan laughed. "Well, first of all, there won't be any TVs."

"That's a great start." I smiled and nuzzled into him for warmth.

I don't know what it was about this guy, but I felt comfortable around him. We may only have had our first official date tonight, but having his arms around me just felt so normal. There was this physical comfort between us that seemed to have been there from the beginning, and I was slowly realizing how often I had found myself in his arms these past few days.

Which was funny, given the fact that I can barely look into his face without blushing like a little girl.

"I don't know where I'll take you, but I promise, after tonight, that it will be extremely boring and normal."

"Boring and normal," I repeated. "Perfect."

Oh yeah, I was really looking forward to boring and normal.

www.ingramcontent.com/pod-product-compliance
Lightning Source LLC
Chambersburg PA
CBHW031725170626
46808CB00005B/1894